Hot Work in Fry Pan Gulch

Honey Beaulieu is cheeky as all get out, a wonderful new heroine in the old west with a singular voice all her own, provided by the extremely capable pen--or computer--of one Jacquie Rogers. Even the title, HOT WORK IN FRY PAN GULCH has a charm all its own. A must-read first book in a new series."

~ **Robert J. Randisi**

author (writing as J. R. Roberts) of The Gunsmith series – 412 novels and counting – as well as the Rat Pack Mystery Series and many others

"A rough and rowdy, Old West tale of shoot 'em up fun and laughs! Watch out outlaws, there's a new Bounty Hunter in town and Honey Beaulieu is a crack shot. *Hot Work in Fry Pan Gulch* is like Annie Oakley meets The Quick and the Dead."

~ **Ann Charles**

USA Today Bestselling Author of the Award-winning Deadwood Mystery Series

"Loved the first story in this new series. It's a fact that nothing is sweeter than Honey. She'll seize your interest while she captures her prey—you'll root for her on every page. I can't wait for the next book!"

~ **Caroline Clemmons**

author of the Men of Stone Mountain series, the Bride Brigade series, and many more

"Fans of Rogers' Western Historical Romances may recognize Honey Beaulieu as the heroine of the Dime Novels eagerly devoured by her Hearts of Owyhee heroines. This is the real Honey, living in the unvarnished West, and filtered through Rogers' unique sense of humor. Reading a book this much fun is downright illegal!"
~ **Judith Laik**, author of The Unsuitable Bride series

"Hot Work in Fry Pan Gulch kicks off a fun and lively new series featuring one of the freshest characters to ever saddle up in the Old West and ride straight into the reader's heart. Honey Beaulieu, Man Hunter, is a winner!"
~ **Wendy Delaney**, author of the Working Stiffs Mystery series

Honey Beaulieu - Man Hunter
Book 1

Hot Work in

Fry Pan Gulch

by

Jacquie Rogers

Camp Rogers Press

Hot Work in Fry Pan Gulch
Honey Beaulieu – Man Hunter #1

Camp Rogers Press

Cover art and design by Chase Miller
Edited by Elizabeth Flynn

Glossary

Just in case you run across a word you don't think is a word...

My poor editor had quite a time with this story—she did her best to preserve the vernacular while keeping me in line (hard enough!), making sure the story is readable to those who aren't accustomed to reading western stories. Keep in mind that grammar as we know it today wouldn't have been correct two hundred years ago, and many of those born in the western frontier missed out on the new way of speaking back East. So Honey's language is perfectly correct for her time and location.

And now, for a few fun words and their definitions as I used them. (I can add to this list any time. If you'd like a word or phrase included, send an email to jacquierogers@gmail.com with the subject HONEY'S WORDS.)

Bellering – vernacular for bellowing

Clumb – climbed

Cribs – a series of small cabins, each barely large enough for a cot and a potbelly stove, where prostitutes who're no longer young or healthy enough to work in brothels can take customers

Get-around (git-around) – body movement; or sometimes refers to stiff hips and knees

Sit-down – one's backside

Hobble – to tie a horse's front legs so they can walk and graze, but can't get too far from camp

Lawdogging – being a peacekeeper (lawdog). Can refer to

any level—local, state, or federal

Loogy – a wad of mucous

Lucifer – a safety match. There were several brand names but most people called them lucifers.

Pure-dee – (pronounced pyur-DEE) emphasizes the following word, as you would use "utter." (That's pure-dee nonsense.)

Owlhoot – criminal, generally a felon, or at least a person of low moral character

Peacemaker – Colt Single Action Army pistol, the gun that won the West, first manufactured in 1873

Pull leather – grab the saddle horn, something no good rider would ever do

Roostered (up) – drunk

Shanny – person of questionable intelligence and/or morals

Spraddle-legged – legs splayed wide

Stock the deck – "stack the deck" is used in the 20th Century, meaning the dealer places cards in the deck to his advantage. However, George Devol always wrote "stock the deck" in his *Forty Years a Gambler on the Mississippi*, and he was in business during the mid-1800s.

Weaner pig – a piglet that's been weaned from nursing, usually at six to eight weeks. They're fast little critters, and cute, too, but they find all kinds of trouble if not properly penned.

Well-heeled – heavily armed, for example carrying a pistol or two, a rifle, maybe a shotgun in the scabbard, and a knife

Dear Reader

I couldn't be happier that Honey Beaulieu's story will finally be told. She's been waiting in the wings for over eighteen years—and not all that patiently, I might add.

Her wait is the story of my writing career. I began writing in 1996 when I dreamed a story. That manuscript wasn't completed until two years later. About three chapters from the end, characters and situations for other books began swirling in my head, which sure didn't help to get that first book finished.

One of my critique partners told me to type them up and put them in an Ideas folder, which I did. I think of it as my own private treasure chest. Many of those ideas developed into books—all the Hearts of Owyhee books came from that, as did Sleight of Heart.

But one of the ideas—my favorite—I knew I'd never write because the large publishers (the only option then) would never in a million years buy a non-traditional Western with a female protagonist that didn't have enough romance to be a Romance, didn't have enough paranormal to be a Paranormal, or enough mystery to be a Mystery, and at that time, there weren't any female action/adventure protagonists.

So this idea stayed in my treasure chest, but every once in a while Honey pounded on the lid. I never forgot her, but writing a book takes a very long time and a lot of commitment of resources, so writing an unmarketable book wasn't in the cards.

Then, last year, Ann Charles and I were discussing where I should go with my next series. For some reason, Honey banged on the lid of the treasure chest again. Only I have to admit, her name was originally Pansy. She always did hate her name, which is why I changed it in the first reference to her in *Much Ado About Marshals*, and she hasn't complained since.

So for the first time since 1998, I opened the file and sent it to Ann. She loved Honey right off the bat, almost as much as I did. She pointed out that we don't have to write to someone else's specifications—I can write anything I want! Furthermore, she convinced me that my readers would love it.

I was excited so didn't tell her my misgivings—at least, not many of them. But I worried that my readers wouldn't go for the grittiness or the more bawdy tone. Even so, once I got all the books that I'd committed to writing off my plate, Honey took stage, front and center. She's not wanting to move off, either.

In my initial concept back in 1998, Honey and her two sisters were all pistoleers. Over time, she brought me around to her way of thinking—this series was hers and no one else's. Her sisters' personalities or occupations haven't changed but they aren't pistoleers, and the series is definitely all Honey's.

So please enjoy the ride along with Honey Beaulieu. She's quite a gal.

Jacquie

Dedication

To Claudia Stephan and Brenda Randolf.
The world needs more people like you.

Acknowledgments

Isn't the cover fantastic? It's the first cover by artist Chase Miller. He drew Honey based on a photo of my granddaughter, and he did an exceptional job. I'm very pleased that Chase is doing the covers for the series.

My editor, Elizabeth Flynn, deserves a war medal for editing this book, what with all the vernacular stabbing her in the heart. She's a trooper, however, and bore up under pressure well. I'm lucky to have her for an editor and a friend.

Honey's beta readers also deserve a medal—they had no idea what they were getting into! Thank you all.

Special thanks to my circle of friends who are there to help me whenever I stumble, which is often.

I'm forever grateful for my reader friends, especially the Pickle Barrelers, who enthusiastically share tidbits about my books on social media, write reviews and post everywhere, and who always lift my spirits. I swear, you guys are go-juice for the soul.

Hot Work in Fry Pan Gulch

Honey Beaulieu – Man Hunter

by Jacquie Rogers

Chapter 1

How I Ended Up Working For Marshal Fripp

1879 – Fry Pan Gulch, Wyoming Territory

"Honey's too scrawny to whore—and damned smart, too—so you need to hire her to rid yourself of that there paperwork you curse to the devil."

That was my mama, owner of the Tasty Chicken Emporium. She served as business manager, madam, and in days past, working girl.

Mama crossed her arms and glared at Marshal Fripp as she tapped her toe. I was nervous as all git-out. Couldn't decide if I wanted him to say yes, or no. The money sounded good, especially if I didn't have to earn it on my back, but I hadn't ever lived on that side of the fence.

"I dunno." The marshal leaned back in his chair and propped his boots on the desk, strewn with all manner of papers—some printed, some with scribbles, and more than a few wadded up.

"Honey does know. She'd have this mess cleaned up inside of an hour. Besides, if you don't hire her, I'm limiting you to only one free visit a week."

He surely enjoyed his three free pokes a week. Sometimes he even paid for extras. One thing about tending bar at the Tasty Chicken—I knew the particulars of what every man in this lousy town liked to do with women.

Two or three times, when the train brought more visitors than normal and Mama was shorthanded, or short-pussied to be more on the mark, I helped out. But I'd only do it regular. None of that peculiar stuff for me.

So that's how I ended up working for Marshal Fripp.

You could say I'm a mite scrawny. That comes from my papa's side. He's tall and rangy, and handsome, too. I expect that's why he was Mama's one and only once they'd two-stepped. They never married, though. Papa's a pistoleer, and he said that was no life for a family. Well, I got news for him—a whorehouse ain't no picnic, either.

It's been a month since Mama hauled me into the marshal's office. Took me three weeks to scrub the whiskey, coffee, and other unidentified dried liquid that I didn't want to know what was off the floor and his desk.

Some of the papers stuck. He didn't have no idea what half the papers was for. I found a coffee cup that he'd been missing for six months and a set of false teeth that he didn't know was there. Said they ain't his, so I screwed them on the privy door for a handle.

Finally, I picked out the wanted posters, leastways the ones that hadn't stuck to the wood, and threw the ripped and wadded papers in the burn barrel.

Then I got out the mop bucket and a good stiff brush. The place smelled a whole lot better once I got the floor and walls scrubbed with lye soap. Marshal Fripp didn't seem to notice one way or the other. Since he made himself scarce the biggest share of the time, I purtied up the office the way I wanted it, although he wouldn't tolerate posies on his desk. That was an easy fix—I went and bought my own danged desk.

The more I did around the office, the less often he was there. Said he had rounds. Lots of those rounds involved a working girl's begonias at the Tasty Chicken. It made no nevermind to me, though, on account of it was a lot more peaceable when he was elsewhere.

Until the mayor came in with the tax papers.

Mayor Tench had a shiny bald head except for two hairs that he combed from his right ear to his left ear, then glued down real good with pomade. What he lacked on top, he made up for with the bushiest mustache I ever did see. No wonder his wife was such a grump.

"Tell Marshal Fripp to collect these monies from the town businesses." The mayor handed me at least twenty papers. "The last city council voted to collect taxes twice a year."

Likely they needed the money to pay their whore bill. "I'll give these to the marshal when he comes in."

"When's he due?"

"I expect when he's done with his rounds, he'll be in." I knew exactly where to find him, and what he'd be doing. My only surprise was that the mayor hadn't seen him there. The girls said the mayor liked it by mouth. I shuddered at the thought.

"I want that money collected by the end of the week."

"Yes, sir. I'll see that the marshal gets your message."

"And the papers."

"I'll see to it myself."

"See that you do."

That man always had to have the last word, so I didn't dare say good-bye when he left, lest he repeat himself.

Just about quitting time, the marshal ambled in like a

satisfied cat. I handed him the papers and he gave them right back.

"Take care of it."

"You mean you want that I should go collect? I'm supposed to be your office help."

"Well, now you're a tax collector."

"Do I get a raise?"

"Let's put it this way—you won't get fired."

* * *

Come Friday, I had all the money collected except for Wakum's Gunshop. "The mayor said if you don't pay, he'll slap a lien on your business."

Wakum glanced at the holey tent walls. "Hell, it's leanin' now."

"Ought I send the mayor in to explain things?"

He cocked the pistol he was cleaning. "He can talk to the end of the barrel, for all I care."

Now, it didn't seem right that all the other business owners had paid up, and naturally the marshal was nowhere to be found, so collecting the taxes from Wakum would take a little different tactic. My brown calico dress and bonnet didn't fit my plans.

One thing he didn't know was my papa had learned me a thing or two, more than most women, or men for that matter, ever knew about shooting. So I went back to my room at the Tasty Chicken and changed to my practice clothes—buckskin britches, flannel shirt, a vest with pockets for cartridges, and my gunbelt.

Papa had given me his old Peacemakers but they were still in fine condition, oiled up plumb nice, and worked slick as a daisy. I slipped them into their holsters at my hip, tied down, and set off for Wakum's place. We was gonna have us a set-to and it would end with me collecting the tax money he owed. That's the way it was gonna be.

Twenty minutes later, I walked back into Wakum's tent and stood at the ready. He never paid a bit of mind to me and continued polishing a pistol. All right, then—I'd wait.

After a spell he said, "State your business." He still hadn't looked up yet, and I couldn't see his face for the brim of his beat-up old Stetson.

"I come to collect the taxes."

"Ain't paying."

"Then I'm taking you in."

Finally he looked at me, a flash of surprise giving him away. Papa always told me every man had a tell. Some hid theirs better than others, but they all had one, and your life could depend on whether you could read it right.

"I came here for three dollars and fifty cents."

"Little miss, I told you I'm not paying."

Well now that pissed me off—not just the "not paying" part, but especially the "little miss" part. I'm scrawny, but I'm tall as the average man. Tall as Wakum, maybe taller. I take after Papa in that regard.

"Then come with me, Mr. Wakum. You're going to jail."

"I'm staying right here. Now go on with you."

"When I leave here, either you'll be headed to jail, or I'll have your three dollars and fifty cents. Your choice."

"You're barking up the wrong tree, little miss." He pointed the pistol he'd been working so hard on and cocked it.

I didn't waste no more breath. In a flash, my gun hand pulled and fired. His beat-up hat now had a nice round hole in it.

"Shit criminy, girl!" Then he smirked. "You missed."

"I didn't miss." I held my Colt on him. "Dead men can't pay taxes, and you needed a new hat anyway."

* * *

"Well, I'll be a skunk's cousin." Mayor Tench looked mighty satisfied as he leaned back in his fancy leather chair on wheels, then glowered at Marshal Fripp before turning his attention to me. "This is the first time all the tax money has been collected on time."

I felt as awkward as a chicken in a duck pond. "Thanks, sir." My mama did teach me manners, even if we lived in a whorehouse.

Marshal Fripp squirmed in his chair, more than likely doing his best not to look hung over. I knew he'd stayed the night at the Tasty Chicken because we both left at the same time that morning.

The mayor tapped his forefinger on the desk. "I'll raise your pay by two dollars a week."

Suited me fine. Seven dollars went a lot farther than five.

Marshal Fripp scooted forward on the seat of his chair, cocked his head, and raised an eyebrow. "Just where you gettin' that two dollars a week?"

"From the marshal's budget, of course." Tench lit his pipe and puffed on it. "You're supposed to have a deputy, not an office clerk, but you didn't get one because you wanted to keep all the money for yourself."

"That's on account of we don't need a deputy. Ain't

nothing going on in this town that I can't handle."

"Nothing other than tax collecting." The mayor got up and came at me with the deputy badge. My legs told me the smartest thing to do was cut and run, but I didn't heed the warning. "Do you aim to see folks abide by the law?"

"I expect so."

He pinned the badge to my brown calico dress. "Then you're deputy marshal. Congratulations."

I had a sneakin' hunch that his congratulations weren't exactly a blessing, but I managed to coerce my lips into a weak smile. Or it might've been a grimace. Not much difference in that sorry situation. I could just imagine the whole danged town making fun of a lady deputy.

"It's a pure-dee waste of city money," the marshal said.

The mayor sat in his chair and picked up his pipe. "Maybe I should recommend that the city contract with the county sheriff for law enforcement services." He pointed the pipe stem at Marshal Fripp. "Then you'd have more time to spend at the Tasty Chicken."

Land sakes alive! I really didn't want to listen to those two go at it, so I stood and jockeyed for position to get the heck out of the line of fire. "Speaking of clerk, I got papers to shuffle." I grabbed the doorknob and yanked the warped door open, feeling two men glaring at my backside—the mayor feeling smug because he'd one-upped the marshal, and the marshal scowling as if he'd just lost his left nut.

"By the way," Fripp called as I was nearly out the door, "the deputy is the official tax collector."

Well, that done it. The two extra dollars would come in handy, but I'm more of a mind with Wakum when it comes to taxes—either the paying or the collecting.

I went back to the marshal's office but Fripp didn't. I reckoned he'd gone straight to the Tasty Chicken. I swear, that man spent more time at the whorehouse than I did, and I lived there.

But not for long. I seen a "For Rent" sign on a tiny house not three blocks from the marshal's office. I didn't have a stick of furniture or even a bedroll to put in it, but I'd lived in a whorehouse long enough. My mind was made up—after work, I'd go rent that place.

The fire bells clanged and the ground shook with hoof beats. I hurried to the window and saw the fire wagon headed down the street so like the good deputy I was, I followed it.

Right to that cute little house.

Chapter 2

Ain't Nothing Sweeter Than Honey

By the time I ran to the little house, the skirts of my brown calico had wound around my legs and I nearly fell into the bucket when the volunteer fireman handed it to me. And so went my introduction as the town's new deputy marshal.

Flames ran up the sides of the house and leapt through the roof. I could see there was no saving it.

"Throw water on the surrounding buildings," the fireman yelled at me.

"Best you get some men on the rooves," I hollered back. The noise of the fire made hearing hard enough, but talking to someone was next to impossible what with all the people running around and bellering. "I'll get people in line and up the ladder. We'll form a bucket brigade up each of the buildings."

He peered at the badge on my bodice. "The hell! You're the new deputy?"

I pointed to the neighboring building. "Haul your ass up there. Now."

It took some doing but I managed to get three other men on threatened rooftops and four lines for people to pass buckets. We was short a ladder so I sent some women to the hardware store to fetch one, plus all the buckets they had in stock.

The water tank was half full but wouldn't be for long, so I sent a couple men to fetch a team and wagon from the livery and put a stock tank in it to haul water up from the creek.

What with the dry weather and the hot sun beating down on the exposed wood, we'd have us a grand bonfire in no time if even one of the surrounding buildings caught fire. We passed buckets of water until we thought our arms would drop off, then we passed some more.

I cursed those damned long skirts more than once. Clothes like that work all right in the house, but they ain't worth spit for fighting fire. A time or two, cinders fell on my skirts and I had to beat the fire out. The thick smoke made it hard to get a good breath, and we all flagged some for the heat.

By the time the water tank in the fire wagon ran dry, the men had come back with the stock tank full, so I sent them back to the creek to fill the fire wagon tank.

"Where's the marshal?" The man who spoke had occasionally bought the cheap services at the Tasty Chicken and wasn't known for hard work. By the look in his eye, I reckoned he wanted to stay, but I'd given him his marching orders to refill the tank. Fripp was most likely at the whorehouse, but that wasn't for them to know.

"I'm in charge here and there's no time to argue. Now git!"

They scowled at me but they done it. Sometimes the disaster at hand is more important to deal with than a scrawny woman yelling orders.

Two hours later, the cute little house was a pile of smoking ashes but we'd saved the other buildings—and the town.

Marshal Fripp strutted up beside me and proceeded to give orders on the mop up as if he'd been there all along, and of course the newspaper reporter talked to him, which was more than fine with me. I knew Fripp would get all the credit.

He could have it—I just wanted a bath. I was bushed. My arms ached and my legs felt like noodles that had been boiled for three days.

"I'm going home." I handed my bucket to the marshal.

"You're not off for another two hours."

"Wanna bet?" I turned away from him before he could spout any more useless blather and headed for the Tasty Chicken. First I'd get me a nice long soaky bath and then put some food in my belly. A week's worth of sleep sounded mighty good, too.

Mama met me at the door. "I heard there was a fire at Widow Stevenson's place."

"Yep."

"You look a fright." She tutted some as she put her arm around me and led me to the bathing room—as if I couldn't find it myself. I expect she was trying to be motherly. She did that every now and again. "You didn't fight that fire, did you?"

"Not by myself. A lot of folks helped and the fire wagon got there lickety-split."

"Is the fire out?"

"Yep, but the house is gone. The other buildings didn't catch, though."

As we passed by the kitchen, Mama said to Alma, "Heat lots of water and have someone bring a change of clothes for Honey."

"Already filled the tub." The cook shooed us out. "Get a move on before the bath gets cold."

In the wash room, Mama set to unbuttoning my dress, which suited me just fine because I didn't think I could lift my arms that high.

"What the hell is that?" She pointed at my badge.

"I'm Fry Pan Gulch's new deputy marshal." No, I didn't shrug. Was way too tired for that nonsense.

"Shit on a tin pan at sunrise, girl. You can't be a deputy marshal."

"Already am."

"Well, me'n Marshal Fripp are gonna do a little conversating about that."

I stepped into the water and Mama dumped in half a box of lavender. After swishing it around to melt, I sank down in the tub, not caring about Fripp, deputying, or nothing else.

Mama went on about this and that—my ears was done listening. Finally I told her, "You'll have to go holler at Mayor Tench. He's the one who deputized me. Now, would you wash my hair? I think my left pigtail got singed."

"Land a'mighty. What am I gonna do with you?"

I didn't much care, long as she washed my hair. My arms wouldn't go up that far. In fact, I wasn't quite sure how the blazes I'd get out of the tub when the time came. Might just sleep there.

* * *

The next day was my day off. I had some thinking to do as to where to live and whuther I actually wanted to be deputy marshal. If not, how would I make a living? Dang tootin' not at the Tasty Chicken. Mama and the gals had a hard life and surely I could find a better way.

Mama had thrown my brown calico in the rag bag so I wore the blue calico and packed the rest of my things in a trunk I'd found in the attic. Every part of me ached. Fighting fires wasn't for wussies, for sure.

I left the house while the day was young, not having a particular place to go, but thought I'd nose around for someplace to rent. The boardinghouses were full except one, where the snooty owner who catered only to respectable young ladies inasmuch slammed the door in my face. Made me wonder if she'd accept my help if her stupid house caught on fire. Made me wonder if I'd bother putting it out.

On the way back home, the mayor's wife said Fripp was looking for me. By the time I got to the marshal's office, Fripp was there, as were several more of his cronies. It was a regular backslapping party and I found out why when I saw the headline of the newspaper.

Marshal Fripp Saves Fry Pan Gulch

I don't know why he wanted me there, other than to wait on his friends, so I busied myself making coffee, sweeping, and such. I doubt if any of them even noticed my presence and that suited me just fine. But it did gall me some that no one bothered to check the facts.

My sore muscles served as a reminder of exactly what did happen at that fire.

"Run and fetch us some Arbuckles'," the marshal said once his friends finally left. "We're a mite low."

I took some money from the petty cash fund and set

out. On the way back, several fellers—the Walton brothers—blocked the boardwalk.

"I hear tell you're the new deputy, sworn to protect us fine citizens."

I knew Clem Walton from the Tasty Chicken—the girls didn't like him on account of he liked it rough. Too rough. "You heard right."

"Where's your badge?" Clem stepped toward me but I wasn't about to back up, so I stood my ground.

"None of your dang business."

"Ain't no lightskirt what can be a deputy anyhow."

"The hell you say."

He grinned—actually more of a snarl. "But I might be persuaded with a little lovin'."

Over my dead body. "What if I don't give a tinker's dam what you think?"

He raised his arm at his brothers. "Might we ought to convince her that she should care."

Wakum had come up and stood with the Waltons, which worried me a mite considering I wasn't exactly on his good side. And I'd left my Peacemakers at home. Wouldn't do that again.

"Best you take it easy," Wakum told Clem, "unless you want to answer to Fripp."

"Ah, that piece of stinkin' cow pie. He ain't no better than having no law a'tall."

I had to agree with him there. Fripp was good at rubbing shoulders and whoring, but not much else that I could see. Still, this duffer had no right to insult the marshal that way. "He keeps the town safe."

"From nothing. We ain't had a robbing or a killing in

a year."

"I rest my case."

Clem made the mistake of grabbing my arm.

I glared at him. "Get your grimy hand off me."

"Looks to me like you could use a little sweetening up."

"You sure as hell ain't the man to do it, and anyway, ain't nothing sweeter than honey." I yanked my arm away, which didn't feel too good, considering all the buckets of water I'd hauled yesterday.

One of his brothers stepped forward and I saw that the lot of them aimed to have a little fun at my expense.

"Tell you what," I said. "Give me half an hour to change clothes and fetch my iron, and we'll settle this."

"I ain't gonna shoot a woman—got better use of 'em."

"Then let me pass and you go visit the Tasty Chicken—you could use a little sweetening yourself."

Wakum winked at me. "I got an idea. We'll have a shooting match. Y'all meet out back of my shop in half an hour and we'll settle this."

Sounded like a good idea to me. "I'll lay five bucks that I'll whoop the lot of you."

"Take her up on it," Wakum said as he clapped his friend on the shoulder. "I'll lay five on you, Clem."

Now, that didn't make a lick of sense. He knew good and well he'd lose that five dollars, yet he'd given me the very dickens when I tried to collect the three dollars and fifty cents of taxes.

"Let's up the stakes some," Clem said, leering at me. "You lose, I get you for the night." He shrugged. "I lose, you get me for the night."

"Whatever you wanna bet, mister." I held up the bag of Arbuckles'. "I have to take this here coffee to the marshal's office, then stop by home, and I'll be there."

"Without the marshal."

"I don't expect you pay him much mind anyhow, so what do you care?"

His answer was of no import to me so I headed to the marshal's office at a good pace and dropped off the coffee. Fripp hollered at me to boil a pot as I headed out the door. He could make his own bad coffee. I had to prove my worth as a deputy, and I aimed to do it alone.

On the way to my room at the Tasty Chicken, I made up my mind that blue calico skirts and deputying didn't go together so good. Once I collected the money from that feller and his friends, I'd head to the general store and buy some more practical duds—shirts, pants, and boots.

Didn't need chaps and spurs on account of I had nothing to ride, and didn't know how anyway. Horses weren't what they rode at a whorehouse.

Might even have enough to rent a decent-size house.

But first, I had to take care of Clem Walton. And then he'd be my enemy, for no man wanted to be bested by a woman.

Chapter 3

Shooting Is More Than Pulling The Trigger

I may not be good for whoring and no one could accuse me of being decent wife material, either, but my pa taught me how to shoot, and no man was better than him. Not that I'm cocky about it all, it's just that I'm at peace with the one thing I do good. Wakum would set up a fair and honest match.

Marshal Fripp undoubtedly had made his own coffee by now. Lord knows the mess I'd have to clean up once this affair was over. With luck, he and his cronies would stay put in the office, and out of my way. The last thing I needed was an audience.

Mama fussed over me when I came home before my shift was over, shoving a lock of hair out of my eyes and kissing my forehead. I always wondered why mothers thought it was their duty to slobber on their kids' foreheads.

"Did you get fired?"

"No, Mama. Just have a little business to take care of." I left her standing in the lounge and hurried to my room. Blue calico wouldn't cut it in a shooting match so I put on my practice clothes and my Stetson. Then I checked my Peacemakers even though I had cleaned and oiled them just last evening. Pa always told me that my life could depend on the good working order of my pistols. My life wasn't in danger, but a girl did have her pride.

Once I buckled on my gunbelt and tied down the holsters, I slipped the pistols in, adjusted my hat, and took a deep breath. Papa had said a calm mind and a sharp eye would win any battle. This was a shooting match, and not a battle, but it felt like one. I had that nervous antsy feeling, sort of as if we'd be shooting at each other instead of a row of bottles. Maybe I ought to take two or three breaths.

Mama hollered at me as I headed out the door, "Where are you going dressed like that, Honey?"

"Just a little shooting practice. Can't get rusty, bein's I'm the new deputy, and all."

"Lawdogging ain't a fit occupation for a woman."

Now where she got ahold of that, I have no idea, considering she was the one who insisted I work at the marshal's office in the first danged place. "Neither is whoring, but someone's gotta do it."

She came over to me and straightened my shirt. "You're too much like your pa." For the first time, I noticed the crow's feet at the corners of her eyes. Mama look tired and it was early in her day. "You go practice, then," she said. "When you get back, I'd appreciate it if you would help me dye my hair. Them gray hairs ain't good for business."

Thinking about Mama helped calm me down some. She had it a lot worse than me on account of she never had a choice—she had been a whore since she was fourteen years old. While I had been raised in a whorehouse and had even taken a customer or two, we both knew I'd never do it for a living.

Mama wanted me to marry a good man and get away from it all, but my idea was to make my own living. I didn't see where you could count on a man for much of anything. Besides, I had no idea how to be a wife, and I sure didn't look forward to satisfying "husbandly urges." From few times I done it, it wasn't none too pleasant.

So making my own way was exactly what I planned to do, starting with whooping Clem Walton in a private shooting match.

My little chat with Mama made me a few minutes late, so I hurried as quickly as I could without winding myself.

Only thing is, I got hung up when I heard a donkey bray not a block away from the gunsmith's tent. An old prospector was whooping on the poor thing good. Or bad. That poor little donkey couldn't have done anything to deserve those lashes. And truth be told, the one thing that riles me quicker than anything else is when the strong are mean to their underlings—whether man or beast.

"Hold it right there, mister," I hollered as I yanked the whip out of his hand. "That donkey has enough welts to treat as it is."

"Give me that whip."

I didn't know this man—didn't want to, either—but he wasn't about to get his whip back. I flung it across the road and the donkey stuck its nose in my hand as if to thank me.

"Ain't no reason to beat an animal. You best go sleep it off before you mistreat any more of them."

"I'll treat the stupid burro any way I want to. She's mine, bought and paid for just last week." He eyeballed my badge. "I got the papers if you want to see them."

"Papers don't give you a license to be mean to her." The donkey shoved her head under my arm. Seemed dreadful smart for an animal to know who was on her side.

I'd never had any sort of animal, either pet or beast of burden. Too bad I couldn't have this one, although I wouldn't have the slightest notion what to do with her. "I got to get to a shooting match, but don't you let me catch you hitting this animal again."

I headed across the road, snagged the whip without even stopping, and took it with me. I didn't trust that old prospector an inch, and it made my gut churn to leave that poor little donkey with such a brute.

So I was at least fifteen minutes late getting to the knoll behind Wakum's tent. What I saw riled me up considerable. Wakum would have to answer for this nonsense.

At least two hundred men lined the shooting range, including Mayor Tench, Marshal Fripp, and all their pals. A couple of men walked through the crowd holding up twenty-dollar bills and yelled, "Four to one, Clem!" Didn't seem right—they should at least give me even odds.

Then before I could even get to the firing line, I heard, "Six to one, Clem!" Now that was downright insulting.

Worse, Fripp and his pals decided to bet on the show. Mayor Tench put money on me, but the rest of them sided with Clem Walton. That aggravated me some, but rather than let it get to me, I wandered over to the bookie.

"Five dollars on Honey," I told him.

"Got it on you? Because I don't take credit. I want cold cash in my palm."

Well, hell. The only five dollars I had was the original bet, and I could be in a world of hurt if I used it for two bets. Not that I'd lose, but folks frowned on such a thing. I turned around but before I got two steps, Mama showed up with her whole posse of girls.

"Here's a five, baby girl." She slipped me the money and I headed back to make my bet. Mama went to talk to the other bookie. She might be a whore, but she knew a good bet when she saw one. Trouble is, the amount of money she shoveled out made me a mite nervous. What if old Clem did out-shoot me?

Mama came back to the firing line and with a practiced hand, snapped her fan open. Once she had her face shielded, she murmured, "Don't you even think about not winning, Honey. Just relax and fire as if your papa was here talking you through it. You know you can whoop old Clem Walton."

"Lot of people here." A dozen deep the men were, all along the roped-off section behind the firing line. Even men from the train, including railroad workers, had come to bet.

"Just remember," Mama whispered. "Clem has a little bitty dick."

I grinned, not knowing if Clem's dick was dinky or not, but Mama did put me at ease. "You'll get your money back and then some," I told her.

"Are you ready?" Wakum called.

I shouldered my way to Wakum, ignoring Clem Walton. "Damn straight."

"Ready to give me a roll in the hay?" Walton sneered at me and I wanted to slap that nasty look right off his face, but getting mad would hinder my shooting.

"If you get any tonight, you'll have to shell out for it." I checked my pistols for the final time, then holstered them.

Wakum hollered at the folks near the targets to clear

out. I seen where he'd set up two rows of ten bottles. No challenge a'tall.

He motioned me and Walton to the firing line. "Five bottles right-handed, five bottles left-handed. You get a point for each bottle, and the shooter who finishes first gets two extra points."

Papa had always made me shoot with both hands but I'd be the first to admit that my right-handed aim wasn't what it ought to be, considering I'm a southpaw. That didn't worry me none because I expected Clem to have the same problem.

"You didn't say I'd have to shoot left-handed," he said, almost a whine.

I stifled a grin. Sure enough, that put him off his stride.

"Them's the rules," Wakum said. "Take it or leave it."

"I'll beat her if I have to shoot with my toes."

Wakum nodded but I noticed a little smile he kept trying to keep at bay. "You all right with the rules, Honey?"

"Fine by me."

"All right then, since Clem's the challenger, he'll go first." He clapped Clem on the shoulder, then took out his pocket watch. "Remember, whoever gets ten shots off first gets two extra points."

"That ain't fair—I only got one pistol so I'll have to reload. Honey's got two."

Wakum shrugged. "Guess you should've thought of that sooner."

Clem needed to be taken down a couple of notches and I aimed to do it, and that wouldn't happen unless we were on even ground. "I'll only use one pistol, if that makes you feel any better."

His answer made no nevermind to me on account of Papa had made me practice reloading nearly as much as we practiced hitting targets. More than once he'd said, "Shooting is more than pulling the trigger." Now I knew what he'd meant. Be prepared. Always. Especially for a grudge match.

Clem started off right-handed and blasted off every one of the five bottles. He fumbled a bit reloading, but made a good show of it. He thought he was tall man at the trough, all right, and he had me bitin' my nails some.

Then he took aim left-handed. Missed the first one, and barely nicked the second one—scooched it over but the bottle didn't fall off. I wasn't sure how Wakum was gonna score that. Clem hit the third bottle fair and square, shot the side out of the fourth bottle but it didn't fall, and missed the last one.

"Eight bottles in thirty-one seconds," Wakum called.

The crowd applauded and then settled down to a low murmur. I glanced around at the satisfied smiles of the men who thought they'd be collecting at the end of the day.

They were hasty in their judgment.

Chapter 4

Five Beans In The Wheel

I had to beat Clem Walton's time and hit nine bottles. Him thinking he could have me easy as that stirred my dander considerable even after I'd made an effort to rope in my mad. For two cents, I'd blast every one of those bottles off the fence so fast, they wouldn't even know I'd shot yet.

A voice in the back of my head said, "Never show your full hand, Honey." It was so real, I turned around expecting to see Papa, only it wasn't his voice I heard. Maybe I was too nervous and riled for my own good, but I reckoned it would be best if I nicked a bottle, same as Clem, and missed one.

"You gonna shoot, or stand there in a stew all damn day?" Clem chuckled as if he was the funniest man ever to set foot on this earth. Which, in a way, he was—in a pathetic way.

"Stall your mug and watch how a woman shoots." I stepped to the mark and drew my pistol with my right hand. I reckoned I'd get the hard part done first, although with the bottles only thirty feet away, it would be hard to miss one. Papa always placed them at fifty feet. Once again, I checked to make sure five beans were in the wheel, then I took aim.

Six seconds, five shots. Five busted bottles—one second faster than Clem, and with my weaker hand, too. If

Papa'd been there, I'd have given him a big hug, except I had reloading to do in a hurry.

That voice said, "Don't fumble, Honey. Keep your movements smooth." All right, then. Loading gate down, revolve the cylinder, remove the casing with the ejector rod, then next chamber, and the next. Five casings out, then put five cartridges in. Close the loading gate. Thirteen seconds—four seconds faster than Clem.

Missed the first bottle on purpose, scooched the second one just like Clem did, hit the third one square in the middle, and nicked the fourth one on the lip but it fell off, so I shot the side of the fifth bottle and it shattered.

Without looking around, I set to reloading.

"Honey wins it," Wakum called. "Collect your winnings, folks. The party's over."

Clem didn't much like his whooping, I reckoned, on account of he shouldered his way through the crowd, followed by his brothers. Either he'd be a worse pest or he'd lay low. My money was on the first.

Mama giggled. "I told you he had a tiny dick; elsewise, he'd have stayed for the party at the Tasty Chicken."

"His dick wasn't pulling the trigger."

"I know, Honey, and we didn't want him, anyway. You beat him fair and square, although you held back some."

"That obvious?"

"Likely not to anyone else, other than maybe the gunsmith. I expect he remembered you're a southpaw from when you shot his hat off." She frowned at the whip hanging from my gunbelt. "What you got that for?"

"Unfinished business. On the way over, I saw some asshole beating a poor little donkey, but since there wasn't time to deal with him proper, I took his whip." Which reminded me to check on the animal—maybe go by the office first and see if any city ordinances could help me throw that lowlife in jail.

Or just shoot the bastard.

"Collect my money from the bookies, Mama. I have some business to take care of."

"You be careful around the Walton brothers. They won't be in good spirits for a while."

Wakum came over, holding a bag of broken glass. "Come see me. I have a few firearms you might like."

"I got two—they work just fine and dandy."

"That they do, but I ain't seen where you've got a rifle or a shotgun."

He had a point there. "Don't need either of them."

"Not until you ride with a posse, *Deputy*."

All right, so he had another point, except I had nothing to ride and didn't know how anyway. "I'll be over after a spell. Thanks."

I left Mama and Wakum, and escaped the crowd, which wasn't too hard since most of the men were a lot more interested in the bookies than me. The marshal's office would be empty on account of Fripp and his friends were all headed for the saloon, and that was fine by me.

Paperwork always waited for me, about the same as dirty laundry—get one pile washed and dried, and another pile of clothes has already started. Just the way of it. But the paperwork could wait. My first job was finding a way to put that mangy donkey owner in jail, or at least fine him a bundle.

Just when I got nose-deep in the city ordinances, I heard gunfire and it sounded close. Sure enough, one look through the window told the story. The very man I wanted to bust to hell tottered in the street, a bottle of coffin varnish in one hand and firing his six-shooter in the air with the other, all the while whooping it up as if he'd just struck gold. Which he might have, for all I knew.

A man like that might not be looking to do harm, but he posed a dreadful danger what with his lack of sense and all. Besides, once he got a good look at me, he wouldn't be in such a partyin' mood.

I drew my pistol and stepped out of the office onto the boardwalk. "Lay your iron down on the ground and back away," I called.

He stopped, wobbled some, then turned my way. "Who the hell are you to tell me what to do?"

"The deputy of this town. I'm arresting you for public drunkenness and firing a weapon in city limits."

"You and what twenty-mule team?" He cackled at his own lame joke. "Speaking of donkeys, you have my whip and I want it back."

"We'll talk about that once you've served your time. Put your pistol on the ground. Now."

He shrugged and laid his six-shooter in the dirt, nearly falling on top of it. But I didn't care about that—I watched his hands, and his right hand went straight for a hideaway gun. Once I saw the barrel, I pulled and shot that sucker right out of his hand.

The prospector howled like a cat with his whiskers afire. "What in tarnation did you do that for?" He held his bleeding hand with the other and staggered backward a step. "I'm going to see the doc."

"No, you ain't. You're going to jail. I'll fetch Doc once you're tucked in and cozy."

"You're a hardass female what needs to learn her place."

"Damn straight. Now walk quiet-like into the marshal's office. The cells are to your left and straight back. Don't dawdle."

"And if I don't?"

"Then I'll shoot your other hand so's you'd have a matching set. Deal?"

"Shit, that ain't no deal," he grumbled, but he stumbled a few steps in the right direction.

"I ain't got all damn day." I cocked my Peacemaker and that got his attention. Nothing sounds quite like a Peacemaker.

"Can I keep my whiskey?"

"Depends on how charitable I feel once you're locked up. If you behave yourself, we'll see what Marshal Fripp has to say on the matter. Elsewise, I'll pour it out right in front of you." I kept a close watch on his good hand on account of he likely had an Arkansas toothpick stashed in that buckskin coat of his.

About the time I got him in the jail cell but not locked yet, Mama showed up. "I heard shots. Got trouble?"

"Had. Still need some help, though. How about I hold bead on this feller while you pat him down. Not the Tasty Chicken kind of patting down, either. Empty his pockets and make sure he doesn't have knives or guns hidden. *Anywhere*."

"You mean for me to check his privates."

"I do."

"I generally make roostered-up maggots take a bath first." But she dove in like an otter in a trout pond.

The prospector squawked when Mama poked his cojones. "Now ladies, that just ain't necessary."

Mama pulled out a derringer, set it on the floor, and scooted it my direction. She kept looking and didn't find any big blades, but he did have an eating knife in his vest pocket. "You want his gold, too?"

"Robbery!" he bellered.

"Take it. I'll record the weight and put it in the evidence locker. Take his papers, too, if he has any, and his suspenders."

"My britches will fall down."

It didn't much matter while he was parked in jail. "I expect that paunch of yours will hold them up just fine."

"You ain't got nothing to hide, anyway," Mama added. She backed out of the cell carrying all she'd found while I coaxed him to the far wall with a wave of my barrel.

Once we had him locked in the cell, he rushed to the bars and grabbed hold, then ran his mouth for a good ten minutes. Mama and me went out to the office and she gave me my winnings, which counted out to over thirty dollars. Mama had made a killin' since she bet five times what I did. Even so, I never had thirty dollars all at one time in my whole life.

"There ain't no call to treat me this way," my prisoner yowled. "I's just havin' me a little fun. Wasn't hurting no one."

Maybe I had been a little hard on him but he deserved

no less after beating that little donkey. "You stay here," I told Mama. "I'm going back for a little chat."

"Want me to back you up with the pistol?"

"No need, but if you see Wakum walk by, tell him I need him."

The drunk was still hanging onto the bars when I got back to the cell.

"How much would you sell that donkey for?" I asked before I'd thought this through, which was a failing of mine.

"Twenty dollars."

"For a donkey? Hell, I can buy a horse for that."

The old geezer sneered. "A nag."

"Still, a nag is a horse, not a donkey."

"Twenty dollars. Firm."

"Best you get some rest. Marshal Fripp ain't due back until morning."

"Morning! Jay-zuz." He flopped his ass on the cot. Bet that jarred his innards.

"Maybe tomorrow afternoon if he's busy. Don't worry, I'll feed your animals. Where are they?"

"The livery on the south side of town, but what about my supper—and my whiskey?"

"I expect I should take as good care of you as you take of your animals." I headed to my desk, shutting the door between the office and the jail cells.

Mama shook her head after I told her the donkey story and what I'd like to do with that heartless, no-good sidewinder. "Don't stoop so low, Honey. I'll send Wakum over to keep an eye on your prisoner, then fetch them both some leftovers after the evening rush at the Tasty Chicken is over."

She meant the café part, I hoped, because I sure didn't want to wait until two in the morning for supper. "Thanks. Send some food for me, too."

Before I did anything, I had to write up an arrest report. Likely the prisoner hadn't given me his right name—John Smith—and for sure he didn't give me his right age—twenty-nine—but that was for the marshal and the mayor to piece out.

* * *

Wakum didn't show up until nearly six o'clock, but he carried a big basket that smelled awful good. "Sorry, Honey, but I had customers after the match," he said as he plunked the basket on my desk and opened it. "Seems everyone who bet on you wanted a new pistol. Dang neart ran out."

I took some food back to the cell, then came back to the office and wolfed down my plateful.

"Deputying must be hungry work," Wakum said as he leaned back and rubbed his full belly.

I nodded and stood, tidying up while still chewing my last bite. So was whipping the local bully in a shooting match. "Thanks for coming by. I'll do my chores and catch some sleep. Be back at midnight because you can bet Fripp won't be here until sometime tomorrow, I reckon, and someone has to stay with the prisoner."

"Take your time." Wakum sat in the marshal's chair and plopped his boots on the desk. He looked a lot more like a marshal than Fripp did.

Not for the first time, I wondered what Wakum's story was.

Chapter 5

Respectability Is A Luxury

Not two steps away from the office, who did I run into but Mrs. Tench, the mayor's wife. She'd have looked scrawnier than me if she didn't pad all the womanly places. I could tell because she wasn't always the same size up top, and sometimes her bustle drooped on one side.

She stopped, resting her parasol on her shoulder, and eyed me up and down. Then again, it's a wonder she could see at all with that big old nose of hers obstructing the view.

"Miss Beaulieu, it's scandalous enough for you to horn into a man's world, shooting and such, without dressing in such an unseemly fashion."

My britches had seams. So did my shirt. Ain't no arguing with her, though. No other female in town wore britches, but some of them could shoot—it was a necessity for the ranch and farm wives.

"I have to fetch the doctor, so if you'll pardon me—"

"There's no excuse for a fallen woman to prance around town in men's clothes."

She wouldn't be satisfied with anything I had to say, so I stepped aside, giving her the full boardwalk to pass.

"Don't you have anything to say for yourself?"

Seemed to me she was plenty willing to do the talking for me.

"I plan to bring this up at the sewing circle." She stuck her nose in the air. "We'll have you fired in no time."

I shrugged and backed away. That woman could out-poison a rattlesnake. "I have work to do, ma'am."

With her eyebrows raised—maybe she thought I'd be easier to sucker into a pissing match—she said, "Well, I never!"

Which was obvious, considering how much time Mayor Tench spent at the Tasty Chicken. But the prisoner's bloody hand needed to be checked and so did that poor little donkey. "Excuse me, ma'am. I have an ass to look at."

She sucked in a gallon or two of air but before she could let loose, I hightailed it to Doc's. He wasn't in so I left a note, then headed to the livery.

"How's John Smith's donkey getting along?" I asked Wheat. He owned the livery, and if a body wanted to rent horses and rigs, or buy—even oxen, mules, and burros—Wheat was the man to see. He also was the best blacksmith and farrier in town. A mite surly, though, on occasion. Wheat didn't cotton to men who didn't pony up when the bill came due. Truth be told, he liked the animals a whole lot more than he liked his customers.

"John Smith?"

"That old prospector. Before the shooting match, I stopped him from whipping his little donkey. Afterward, he danced in the street with his booze and firing his six-shooter every which a'way, so I arrested him."

"His name's Ed Roxbury. I doctored up his burro some. She ain't hurt too bad—oughta be healed up fine in a few days."

"By then, he'll be lashing her again. I sorta shot his right hand and threw in him in jail. That'll slow him down some."

Wheat grunted his agreement, then motioned me to follow him. "Want to see her?"

He led me out of the main barn to a shed on the side. "Her left ear's messed up some."

There she stood, the sweetest-looking critter, all lop-eared and chewing straw. Why she ate straw when she could've eaten the hay in her manger, I wouldn't dare to guess. "She's skin and bones."

"It oughta be against the law for a man like that to own an animal," Wheat said. "For two cents, I'd take the bastard out and shoot him myself."

I was tempted to see what he'd do for a nickel, but held my counsel. The donkey came right up to me and nuzzled my hand, so I scratched her wherever she didn't have sores.

"You're a nice girl," I cooed, and she rubbed her head along my ribs.

When I stepped back, thinking maybe she didn't want me in her pen, Wheat said, "Let her pet on you. She likes you."

"Maybe I should buy her."

"Tell you what, since old Ed's likely a mite sore at you, I'll see if I can work a deal without him knowing who the buyer is."

"Said he wanted twenty dollars."

"Five dollars, more like it."

"That's what I thought, but he knows I'll pay more just to see her heal up and be happy."

After I petted the donkey for ten minutes or so, I left

and headed to the Tasty Chicken. Things weighed on my mind. I needed a place to live. Mrs. Tench's criticism still stabbed me in the heart even though every word was true. But no denying it, I was sure enough raised in a whorehouse, and I sure enough wore britches. Respectability was a luxury I'd never have, so there was no use moaning about it.

And that donkey needed a home. I could hardly keep her in my upstairs room. No doubt, I'd do my best to buy her—not that I had any idea what I'd do with a donkey. And after winning the shooting match, I had the money but I'd be damned if I'd line that bastard's pocket.

Mama promised to wake me at eleven-thirty, so I went to my room for a few hours of shut-eye. That ain't easy what with all the goin's-on in a whorehouse, but I was used to it. More what bothered me was all the yammerin' in my head because one way or another, I had to make a living, and I didn't want to have to worry about all the Mrs. Tenches in the world.

* * *

At midnight, I spelled Wakum, who'd cleaned every firearm in the office for lack of anything to do.

"Fripp needs the firing pin replaced on that old Henry," he said as he stood. "I'll see you tomorrow."

"The prisoner's name is Ed Roxbury."

"I know. And he's fifty-eight years old."

"How'd you find that out?"

"He was carrying a Schofield revolver that I sold a few years ago to a rancher, and I wanted to know if 'John Smith' had stolen it. Turns out, he just bought it a week ago and the bill of sale is with his personal effects."

I felt a little stupid for not checking the papers in his pocket, and next time, that'd be the first thing I'd do. I scratched out *John Smith* and wrote in *Ed Roxbury* on the report, and asked, "Did he mind his manners?"

"I gave him his bottle back. You won't be having any trouble from him tonight."

Wakum left and Roxbury was sawing logs, so I locked the front door, put the keys in my pocket, and tried to make myself comfortable in the other cell. The cot had lumps the size of a buffalo and between that and the prisoner's sleep serenade, I didn't get in a wink of shut-eye, but did do a lot of thinking.

What I knew about lawdogging could be written inside a locket. What started as an office helper had blown up past all my experience these last few days, and all on account of Wakum not wanting to pay his damned taxes. I didn't know whether to shoot him or thank him. First off, he gets me hired as deputy, then he wrangles me into that confounded shooting match. And on top of it all, I'd likely own a donkey before long.

Maybe a place out of town would be better, although what all that involved mystified me. Living in a whorehouse hadn't given me a whole lot to go on in the rest of the world.

The world. I'd spent most of my time within three blocks of the Tasty Chicken. Sorta made me wonder what all I was missing.

* * *

The next morning, closer to noon, actually, I sat at my desk shuffling papers when Marshal Fripp came in all red-nosed and surly. His night out on the town hadn't done him any favors.

"A prisoner?" he hollered. "You can't just go arresting every man who gets drunk. Meals come out of the budget, you know, and there ain't much in the budget now that I have to pay you."

"He was causing a ruckus."

"What did you charge him with?"

"Public drunkenness, shooting in town, and resisting arrest."

"Hell, they all resist arrest." He pointed to the stove, indicating that I should fetch him a cup of coffee. "How many folks do you know that want to be arrested?"

"And he's mean to his donkey." I put the coffee on his desk—black, strong, and hot. "How long until the judge gets here?"

"Can't afford to wait for the judge—he's a moron anyway."

"The judge? Or Roxbury?"

Fripp ignored my remark, which was just as well. "I'll fine the feller five dollars before meal time and let him loose." The marshal shook his finger at me. "And don't you go arresting no one else without telling me. Costs money."

"Yes, sir." I handed him the paperwork. "I best be on my way, then. My bed is callin' my name."

"I'll expect you bright and early in the morning to make up the hours." He slurped his coffee.

"I stayed here all night guarding the prisoner—"

"That you shouldn't have arrested."

"The five-dollar fine will cover his meal and then some. You might even have enough left over for an hour at the Tasty Chicken."

"Get out of here. And you better be at your desk when I get here tomorrow."

That wouldn't be a stretch—I was always at the office before he came in. I headed straight for my bed, all right, by way of the livery on the other side of town. On the way, I looked for "For Rent" signs but didn't see any. Maybe Wheat would know where I could rent a place for myself and the donkey that would soon be mine somehow or another.

A few minutes later, I walked into the livery. Wheat was shoeing one of the finest horses I ever did see—a big sorrel with a blaze and three socks. Any man would be proud to ride such a horse as that.

"Where'd you get this fine gelding?" I asked.

"Ain't mine—belongs to the U.S. deputy marshal." Wheat kept right on filing the horse's hoof.

"This is a territory. I didn't know U.S. marshals cared for us one way or another."

"They don't. He was riding through and his horse threw a shoe." He took a new shoe off the wall and placed it on the hoof for measuring, then carried it over to the anvil. "Go on back and visit with the donkey if you want."

"I do, but first I have to tell you that Fripp was none too pleased with me arresting Roxbury. The marshal's going to fine him five bucks and let him loose, so he oughta be by inside of an hour. Fripp wanted him out of there before he had to pay for another meal."

Wheat grunted and I left after casting another admiring look-see at that sorrel. I didn't have far to walk because the donkey came right up to me and brushed against my side, nearly knocking me over. Her withers were about the height of my armpits. I reckoned she was full growed, but I'd have to ask Wheat for sure.

"Take it easy, girl. With a little luck, I can take you home—first I have to buy you, and then we need to find us a place to hang our hats."

The donkey brayed, and I swear she frowned.

"I know you don't have a hat. That's just a sayin'." I glanced to her stall, the gate latched good and proper. "Looks like you're some sort of escape artist."

She wouldn't be herded, led, or dragged back to the pen, but she followed me everywhere else, including back to Wheat. She didn't seem to mind him but she stuck right by my side.

"Looks like she picked her human," Wheat said as he gave the hoof nail one final whack. He set the horse's foot down gently, then stood and stretched his back.

"Yep, and the second floor of a whorehouse ain't exactly the best place for her to live. Do you know of a house for rent?"

He wiped the sweat from his brow, then scratched the back of his head. "I got a room for rent in the loft of the livery, but that ain't a fitting place for a woman."

"That's fine, because I ain't a fitting woman. How much to board the donkey?"

"Four bits a week for the room, a dollar for the donkey."

"I'll go fetch my stuff."

From a whorehouse to a livery. I reckon that's just this side of respectable.

Chapter 6

Not A Lick Of Sense

By the time I got back to the livery with my clothes and what few other belongings I could scare up, Wheat had negotiated a deal with Roxbury. He sold me the donkey for five bucks. I also charged him five dollars for the whip, making it a square trade—the donkey for the whip.

"I'll need two copies of the bill of sale," I told him. "And I want both of them witnessed by Mayor Tench."

"Now ain't you getting a mite carried away, *Deputy* Beaulieu?" Roxbury wanted to make good and sure I knew that he didn't think I should be a deputy, but I paid no mind to him, since it wasn't one damned bit of his business. Truth be known, I wasn't so sure, either.

Wheat patted the side of his hip where a Peacemaker would've been and cocked his head—sort of a half of a nod. I took it to mean I should stick to my guns.

To Roxbury, I said, "You stole everything you could get your grimy hands on this week. You likely stole this donkey, too. When some man comes to town looking for his donkey, I want it on paper that you're the one who sold him to me. Besides, if you don't do it, you ain't getting your whip back, pure and simple."

Somehow my elbow managed to connect with his ribs. It was an accident. Then Wheat picked up some tongs out of the forge and Roxbury's arm ran right into them. Once the old coot got done hollering, he suddenly came around to my way of thinking.

An hour later, I and Roxbury was leaving the mayor's office after we'd signed the papers. He headed straight for Doc's, even walked right by the saloon on the way.

A block away from the livery, the donkey met me. The little turd seemed to know all what happened and was lovin' all over me.

"You need to learn to stay put," I told her. Somehow, I don't think she listened to that bit of advice.

Now I owned my practice clothes, two dresses, unmentionables, one pair of boots, a hat, a bonnet, two blankets, two Peacemakers and gunbelt—and a donkey who went wherever she damn well pleased.

* * *

The room in the loft of the livery purtied up just fine. Can't say as the bed suited me as well as the one in the Tasty Chicken, but the room was bigger and I didn't have to listen to a bunch of men grunt as they did their deed.

Every now and again, a horse nickered, and if I didn't feed Sassafras on time, she'd wake me up with vigorous braying. Shortly after that, Wheat would commence to banging on his anvil. He had quarters at the other end of the livery, over the front door, with a small potbelly stove for heat and boiling coffee, but he only lit the stove in the cold months.

Most times, he ate at Bougie's Saloon two doors down—mostly because he liked to look at Bougie's twin daughters, Julie and Liette—then he'd come back to the livery and boil his coffee over the forge before it got too hot. Sometimes I went to Bougie's with him and had porridge, but generally, I skipped breakfast and went straight to work.

As did my new donkey companion, Sassafras, whose name got shortened to Sassy at about the third saying of it. Sassafras is a mouthful. Marshal Fripp didn't much like her, but then I didn't much like him so I reckoned that made us even.

Sassy couldn't come into the office, of course, but she'd hang around outside, begging treats from anyone who passed by. That beast had no shame. Anytime I left the office, she was right with me, happy as a rabbit in a carrot patch.

I commenced to training her. Once her back healed up, which took about a week, I made her a little pack to carry around so she'd get used to it, and in another week, I'd add a little weight to it. But first she needed to learn to stay put.

That was easier said than done, on account of she wanted to be with me wherever I went. She even tried to climb the ladder to the loft. But in my job, bullets could fly anytime and I didn't want her to catch one, so staying put was an important lesson for her to learn.

"Honey, I want this budget report finished by the time I get back from my rounds," Fripp said as he stood and put on his hat. That man had about as much ambition as a bloated steer, and he farted about that much, too.

"I'll have it done. Enjoy yourself." He'd head straight for the Tasty Chicken as usual. I reckoned he thought he'd find all the town criminals there.

He left and I waded into the paperwork, which didn't take me more than an hour. With a couple hours to kill, I tidied up the place and cleaned the cells just in case we had ourselves an overnight guest.

"Mail!" Thad Ruhl, the mailman and proprietor of the Golden Ruhl Mercantile, called from the front office.

I dried my hands and went to greet him. "Want some coffee?" I asked, hoping he had time to visit a spell. We've known each other for a long time, him being a patron of the Tasty Chicken, but only the saloon and restaurant. I never knew him to partake of the girls.

"Don't mind if I do." He put a wad of large packets on the marshal's desk. "The stagecoach brought me more mail than I normally deliver in a week, so I best be hoppin', but a little coffee might do me some good."

Sassy poked her head in the door after Thad settled in his chair.

"No," I told the donkey. "I can't play with you yet. You'll have to entertain yourself for another few hours."

"Don't you ever tie that critter up?" Thad asked.

"Naw. She never goes very far from me, but I do worry that someone might cotton to such a sweet little donkey and take her home."

"Not much call around here for donkeys. Too small for riding or plowing."

I took the top packet. "I'll start in on this hellacious pile, if you don't mind. This blasted mail ain't gonna take care of itself."

"What you gonna do with that donkey?" He moved into a chair farthest from the stove, bein's the day was hot, and fanned himself with his hat.

"I haven't rightly pieced that out yet, but she seems to think I belong to her so that's the way it is."

"Looks stronger every day. If you ever go on a trip and need a pack animal, she'll do you fine."

"No plans to do such a thing." Hell, I'd never been more than ten miles from Fry Pan Gulch, and then only on rare occasion with Papa.

One packet held a dozen or more wanted posters, two copies of each. I separated them into two piles—I'd nail one of each to the office wall, then give the other pile to Fripp.

"Looks like Fripp will be visiting your store later." The marshal always enjoyed making a production when he posted them at the general store, which doubled as the post office.

"I'll let my patrons know as I deliver the mail so he'll have a good audience. Best I get back to the store first and make sure I have plenty of peppermint sticks and a full pickle barrel for the marshal's show. Besides, the train'll be here in an hour and the travelers only have a few minutes to buy whatever they need." He didn't move out of his chair, though.

I picked up my stack of posters and thumbed through them. "A lot of these hard cases look flea-bitten and haggard—could just be the drawings, though."

"Never knew a man like that to be purty."

"I expect you're right on that score." What caught my eye more than their looks was the amount of the bounties. "Whoo-ee! One of them fellers is worth five hundred dollars. That's a lot of money."

"More'n I ever seen at one time."

I couldn't take my gaze off that paper. Russell Winterborne, aka Ruff Winter. He didn't have much of an imagination if he thought he could fool folks with that alias.

"Damn, Thad. It'd take me a year and a half to make that much at seven dollars a week, most of which I have to spend, what with the price of food and rent." That five hundred dollars stuck in my head. Even if I made my living on my back, it would take six months or more to collect that amount. And the price of making that much money could be a long slow death. I seen it many times.

"You still have to eat, no matter where you are."

I tossed the paper back on the pile with the others. "True, and I expect sleeping on the ground would get old after about, oh, an hour."

"There's something to be said for a soft mattress." Thad took one last slurp of coffee and stood. "Don't you get any fool notions in that head of yours, Honey Beaulieu."

"I ain't planning to. Got enough to do around here." And a donkey to keep out of trouble. "Thought I'd stop by the store later—need some curtains and such."

"Yeah, I heard you rented a room at the livery." He put on his hat and slung his mailbag over his shoulder. "The missus can help you pick out some nice frippery. If I get done with the mail, I might see you. Thanks for the coffee."

He left, but he wouldn't make it back to the store before closing time if he spent as much time visiting as he did delivering. That didn't matter to me none since I reckoned his wife would be more helpful to me anyway.

No sooner had he left but a boy come running in. "There's an awful doin's at the Bougie Saloon! You gotta come—Pa said you better be well-heeled, too."

I buckled on my gunbelt and took a shotgun out of the gun rack. "You best fetch Marshal Fripp. He's likely at the Tasty Chicken. Tell him I'm already on my way, but that I won't make no arrests."

"What if they need arresting?"

"With luck, the marshal will be there by then and he can do the honors."

Before I left, I shooed Sassy into one of the cells and locked her in, since she'd never stay put, especially since Bougie's is so close to the livery. I didn't want her amidst flying lead, and she didn't have a lick of sense in that regard.

She brayed as I ran out, and in fact, even halfway across town I could still sorta hear her hollering at me.

Odd thing about heading square into trouble—my legs told me to go the opposite direction but my head told me I had a sworn duty to uphold the law. Whether I'd find a bit of a dustup or a slaughter, I had no idea, but I was sure hoping for the dustup.

Not for the first time, I wished someone had taught me something about lawdogging. No time like the present to learn. Running all that way left me nearly out of breath and I had to stop to take in some air about the time I got within a block of Bougie's.

A lady screamed and gunfire echoed off the buildings. No time for air! I hauled my butt to the saloon as quick as I could, but stopped just outside the door.

"Hold your fire! Deputy Beaulieu here, and I'm coming in."

A man snickered—more of a guttural, evil laugh.

"Come right in, Deputy Beaulieu. We'll put you next on the entertainment list."

"Never let them get your goat."

I looked over my shoulder to see who'd said that, on account of it was the same voice I'd heard at the shooting match. But no one was there. Again. Sounded like decent-enough advice, though, so I took a deep breath, calmed my innards, and peeked through the window.

Two strangers had got Bougie's twin girls, Julie and Liette, in a bad way. Julie's clothes was torn and she had a bloody lip as she struggled against the man a third again her size who held her. Liette stood at the end of the bar, away from the men. Her cheek looked a deep red and would turn into a hell of a bruise, so they'd already roughed her up some. I also saw that she had picked up a broken table leg and hidden it in her skirts. Smart gal.

The pretty Bougie girls had more sand in them than most men I knew, but they were outnumbered and outgunned, especially without their pa, who sprawled on the floor just in front of the bar, his leg bent unnatural-like. One of the men came at Liette and she swung that table leg as if she was the star home run hitter for the Chicago White Stockings.

While they were distracted, I bolted through the doorway and held bead on the man who wrestled with Liette. "Next man that moves gets a bullet in his gizzard," I yelled.

And I meant it.

Chapter 7

Girls Don't Kill In Cold Blood

Liette swung the table leg with all her strength and clouted the horny scoundrel upside the head. He dropped with a thunk, then she had the good sense to jump astraddle of him and commenced to punching his face and neck—just to double-damn guarantee he wouldn't trouble her no more. The scum had that coming to him, but I had a whole room of rowdies to quell, especially the one who had wrenched Julie's arm behind her back.

I waited for his tell just like Papa told me to do. It worked with Wakum and I had a sneakin' hunch he'd been quite a hellraiser in his younger days—likely a more competent hellraiser than these bottom-feeders.

The sidewinder who held Julie pointed his six-shooter right at me. The hole at the end of the barrel looked awful big on account of me standing at the wrong end of it. But he wobbled some and if he shot me, it'd be by pure-dee accident, so I sashayed to the left where I could get a clear aim at his side, which also made him shoot backhanded.

Without giving him time to piece out what I'd done, I squeezed the trigger. The crack of gunfire nearly deafened me and I admit it put me off-guard some, bein's I'd never fired in a building before. He didn't fall but if I shot the pistol out of his hand like I'd done with Roxbury, it could blow up in Julie's face, so I shot him again in the shoulder.

He let go of Julie and she ran to Liette and helped her sister with the pummeling. Them girls was dang good at it.

The man I shot slumped to the floor, holding his side with his left hand, but still pointing his pistol at me with his right. "I'm gonna kill you, Honey Beaulieu."

"Put that thing down or the next round goes into your eyeball and out the back of your head—and it'd be a pleasure to put it there."

"Girls don't kill in cold blood." He had the nerve to snicker at me, which pretty well made up my mind right there.

"I guess you'll have to try me to find out." I stood solid—him pointing his pistol at me, and me aiming for the kill. "Think it's worth it? Hellfire, I'd like to see for myself. I've killed four-legged varmints and no-legged varmints, but never a two-legged one."

"You talk too damned much." And that's the last thing he said before he plumb gave out. Nap time.

"Walk up to him real ginger-like, Julie, and take his pistol. I don't trust but what he'd come back alive on us."

His friends didn't want no part of any shooting and skeedaddled out of the place like a bunch of wet skunks with their whiskers on fire. And they was damn certain a bunch of skunks, too. One feller even jumped through the window, busting perfectly good glass. I aimed to get him to pay for that.

"Liette, Marshal Fripp is s'posed to be on his way. When he gets here, light out and fetch Doc." I wasn't sure whether to holster my Peacemaker or not but chose not to, just in case the turd woke up and wanted to play dirty again.

Liette shook her head. “Papa needs help, Honey. I don’t give two hoots nor a holler about that worthless Fripp—I’m fetching Doc now.” She took off at a run. I had no doubt that she’d be back with the doctor before Fripp even showed. He’d be noodlin’ for the headline in the newspaper, though. Not a one of us would be surprised if he didn’t bring the reporter along.

“Julie, you got some rope?”

“Twine for wrapping packages.”

“That’ll do. Fetch it and tie up both these fellers.”

“Are you taking them to jail?”

“Nope, can’t arrest anyone without Fripp’s permission—he don’t want to pay for their meals—but he didn’t say a thing about shooting them.”

Julie ran to the back room and returned with a big ball of twine in less than a minute.

“Wind the both of them tight.”

“The one you shot is bleeding.”

“Might have to put a tourniquet around his neck—that oughta stop it.” The Peacemaker felt like it weighed about twenty pounds by now, what with me holding it straight out for so long, but I wasn’t about to take the bead off him. “Hope Fripp gets here soon.”

* * *

Marshal Fripp charged in, pistols drawn. “You can holster ’em now, Honey.” He shoved me aside.

The reporter peeked through the door. “Is it safe?”

“Yep,” Fripp said in a low, commanding tone—should’ve been on stage—still aiming at the two men tied up on the floor. Both of them whimpered something pathetic. “Everything’s under control.”

"Good job, Marshal." The reporter scratched some notes. "Who are the criminals and what happened?"

"They attacked Bougie's two fine daughters, but as you can see, both ladies are all right—just a mite shaken." He scanned the room. "Where's Miss Liette?"

"Gone to fetch the doctor," Julie said.

She started to say something more but I shook my head at her and she hushed up. Fripp loved the headlines, and my life would go a lot smoother if he got them. Plus, the less written about me, the better.

"What are the charges?" the reporter asked.

"No charges yet. We'll wait until Doc checks them, then do all the paperwork."

The reporter scribbled more on his pad, drew a diagram, and left. As soon as the door slammed, Fripp sent me a scowl that could've petrified cow piss.

"I told you not to arrest anyone unless I say so," the marshal hollered.

"I didn't arrest them. I shot them. What you do with those two is no concern of mine."

"We don't have no gawddamn choice since you shot them, and the reporter's gonna be dogging me about it."

Liette ran in with Dr. Peter George behind, carrying his black bag. He went straight to Mr. Bougie, who was coming around, and knelt beside him.

"Quite a lump you have on the back of your head," Doc said after he took Bougie's pulse. He crooked his finger at the twins. "Help me get him into bed. I'll give him something for pain and splint his leg, then I'll check up on him after I get back. Meantime, keep him comfortable and make sure he rests."

I headed for the door but the marshal cocked his head at the spot where I'd stood, so I went back.

A few minutes later, Doc came back into the saloon area. "Which one is hurt the worst?"

"Take your pick." I pointed at the one I'd shot. "He has a couple bullets in him. The other got walloped with a table leg."

"That's some fancy work, Fripp."

The marshal puffed out his chest, then holstered his pistol. "Just doin' my job."

Doc knelt beside the bleeding man and put his finger on the man's neck. After a short spell, he said, "Get me four men to haul these two back to my surgery." He stood and nodded at Fripp. "I'll send you the bill."

The marshal pointed at me, then at the door. I reckoned he wanted me to fetch the men, so I did. That didn't take much doing on account of a whole passel of fellers crowded around the boardwalk, hoping to see what all the hoopla was about. "Four of you strong fellers get in there—Doc needs two men took to his office."

Once four of them hitched up their britches and went in, I left. Fripp didn't need me to water down his glory, and anyway, I didn't think my digestion could tolerate the watching of him strut around like head rooster.

As I walked down the boardwalk, Wakum waved at me from the door of his gunshop, so I went over there. He asked what the shots were about and I told him, then I spent a little while visiting with him and admiring the rifle and shotgun he was just sure I had to have.

"It'd take six months of wages to pay for them," I said.

"Hell, you got most of the money now," he argued.

"You won a bundle off the shooting match."

"Yeah, but I don't know from one day to the next whether I'll have a paycheck what with Fripp ready to fire me every ten minutes."

And I didn't know how much longer I could put up with his bullshit, either, but I reckoned there'd be a good dose of that in any job. Seemed like Fripp dished out more than his share, though.

Wakum smirked. "It does stick in his craw when you show him up."

"That ain't hard to do." I took another admiring glance at the rifle, which I hoped to buy sooner or later. "Best I be on my way. I left Sassy in the cell while I was taking care of business."

By the time I got back to the marshal's office, Fripp was already there.

"What in the ever-lovin' hell is a dadblamed donkey doing in my jail?" I nearly had to cover my ears for all Fripp's bellering. That man needed a dose of laudanum or some such. He plopped in his chair, struck a lucifer, and lit his cigar. Once he'd taken a couple puffs, he scowled at me. "Explain yourself, Honey, or you're out of a job."

"I didn't want Sassy in the way. Seemed like the best way to keep her safe was to lock her in a cell."

"You ever heard of a corral?"

"She don't put much store in fences." I took the keys, headed back to the cell, and unlocked the door. Sassy trotted out and flicked her tail as she passed the marshal, not at all worried about the marshal's snit, I reckoned, because she didn't even look at him. She did leave a present in the cell, but I was prepared for that and scooped it up before Fripp saw it.

"Gonna go get me some dinner," I said as I hurried past the marshal who by then had tipped his chair back and plopped his boots on the desk in his customary manner.

"Make me some coffee, but fetch me a pack of cigars first."

That rankled me some. He could just as well get his own damned coffee and cigars—but to preserve the peace, mostly my peace, I boiled coffee for him. And I didn't even spice it with donkey dung.

* * *

Roxbury didn't seem to cotton to staying out of trouble, and once he found it, he always had what he thought was a good excuse. First he caused a big stink in the Tasty Chicken when he paid for an overnighter, but then stole the cash box. Said he mistook it for his own. I managed to steal it back without arresting him, for I didn't have permission from Marshal Fripp, which pissed me off something dreadful.

A few days later, Thad Ruhl caught Roxbury pocketing goods at the Golden Ruhl Mercantile. Thad dragged Roxbury into the marshal's office. The thief looked worse for the wear, what with his nose leaking and his shirt ripped.

"I caught this son of a bitch stealing."

Fripp stood, stopping Thad from taking his prisoner back to the cell. "What did he take?"

The frowning store owner held up a bag and shook it, still holding the thief by his neck with the other hand. "All this he had stuffed in his pockets. Then he tells me he didn't steal it—I guess it just jumped into his pocket."

"Must be some sort of miracle," Roxbury muttered.

Thad nodded toward the cell. "I want this man jailed."

"Now, don't be hasty. I'm fining him five dollars." Fripp turned to Roxbury. "I want you out of town by nightfall. If I ever seen you in Fry Pan Gulch again, I'll arrest you and throw away the key. You got that?"

The store owner got all in a toot when Fripp told him to let go of his prisoner. "Dagnabit, Fripp. This man needs to be arrested and hauled to court. You can't let scum like him break the law at will." Thad glared at Fripp like he wanted to clock him on the jaw and I couldn't blame him a bit.

When Thad finally let Roxbury go, the smug thief wiped his bloody nose on his sleeve, dug out five bucks and slapped it on the marshal's desk, then made a point of walking right in front of Thad on the way out. More of a jaunt than a walk, actually. Enough to frost the store owner's pumpkin, for sure.

"I'm gonna remember this the next time you want credit, Fripp." He glared at the marshal's chair a moment, then grabbed it and grunted as he slung it on his shoulder. "You haven't paid for this yet. I'm taking it back."

Fripp snorted and growled after he watched his chair leave the office, and about three seconds later, swiped my chair. I'd have to buy another one. That damned Roxbury wasn't worth it. Someone ought to take care of the sticky-fingered turd.

Chapter 8

A Man Like That Won't Stay Afoot For Long

I kept an eye on Roxbury. He grumbled and cursed all the way back to the boardinghouse, and after a spell, came out carrying his war bag on his shoulder. Sassy and me followed him none too quiet-like, and every once in a while he'd look back at us and scowl. We tailed him all the way to the livery where he'd boarded his horse.

Since visiting with Roxbury wasn't appealing, I put Sassy in her stall. She'd stay there because she was hungry—I left her with hay and a sugar lump. On the way up to my room in the loft, Roxbury hollered, "Three dollars! That's robbery!"

Robbery was something he oughta know about, that's for sure. I stepped off the ladder and squatted behind some harnesses so I could see him and Wheat.

"That's for feed, a new shoe on the right front, and doctorin' where you'd been heavy with the lash." Wheat pumped the bellows a few times and then lifted up his red hot tongs as if he hadn't never seen them before. He sure did know how to use the tools of his trade to advantage. Roxbury had ought to piece that out, bein's this was the second time.

"That fleabitten nag ain't worth three dollars." But he stepped back. I knew Wheat would win.

"Neither are you," Wheat said. "But you paid more

than that at the boardinghouse."

I had to stifle a giggle at Wheat's comeback. He wasn't one to mince words.

"Well, shit. You can have the blasted nag, then." Roxbury hitched up his war bag and took off, heading out of town afoot.

Wheat went back to hammering whatever it was he was making—looked like some sort of hinge. I peered out the door, just to make sure Roxbury hadn't made any wrong turns. He hadn't.

"I hope that's the last we've seen of that bastard," I told Wheat.

"Don't count on it lest he find hisself a ride. A man like that won't stay afoot for long."

I hoped he did buy a horse. "I'm gonna go to the Golden Ruhl and buy some duds."

* * *

"Nope," I told Mrs. Ruhl when she held up a nice pink housedress. "I learned you can't mix it up in skirts. Show me some britches and a shirt. Unders, too." I was feeling a mite flush, and it wasn't often I could buy anything for myself. "Might even buy me a new hat and boots."

Half an hour later, I left the store with an armload of clothes more suited to lawdogging. Mama wouldn't be happy, but then she had more common sense than most women, so she wouldn't say much. As for anyone else's opinion, well, I just didn't give a shit.

I also bought a lasso. Don't ask me why—I just wanted one. It cost me two bucks. Let's just say there wasn't much left of last payday. As in none. I even had to dip into my winnings, which I was saving just in case a house came up for rent. Most folks took living in a house for granted, but the only place I'd ever lived was a whorehouse, and now the livery. Of the two, I preferred the livery.

Something about the animals settling down for the night made for a peaceful sleep for me, too. That sounds like pure-dee folly, but that's the way it had been every night since I moved in.

On the way back to the livery, I picked up a crate that someone had kicked to the side of the road. It would make a dandy clothes chest. Next payday, I'd buy me a bowl and pitcher so's I could wash up in my room rather than in the horse trough. I didn't mind washing my hands in it, but cleaning my teeth there was a mite off-putting.

"Shopping, eh?" Wheat barely glanced up from his bellows as I walked in.

"Clothes. Needed some. These britches is getting a mite rich, and dresses don't suit lawdogging—too easy to get tangled up."

"Yep, I'd expect so."

I clumb the ladder, hauling the crate with my new clothes in it. I wanted to be alone so I could admire them in peace, but Sassy stood below, braying her head off. She wouldn't shut up until I gave her a little lovin' so back down I went. She butted me with her head until I'd scratched her ears enough to suit her, which took a while.

"Might as well put a pack on you and we'll take a little tour of the town," I told her. Fripp didn't do rounds in the way a lawman ought, so I reckoned I'd give it a whirl, and work on Sassy's training at the same time.

We ended up at the Tasty Chicken and I tied Sassy up

in the back, right by Fripp's horse. The donkey gave me a nasty look, but dang, she couldn't go in a whorehouse. Would cause all sorts of commotion.

The marshal would be in the bar or the dining room if he wasn't upstairs, so I headed straight for the kitchen.

"Hi, Honey." Mama gave me a big hug and sat me at the table. "You haven't been eating right." She told the cook to bring me a little of the night's special. "We'll have your belly full in no time."

"I'd be grateful for a bath, too."

"The tub's busy all night from all the train travelers, but come over in the morning before work and you can take a nice long bath with no one bothering you."

"Sounds good to me. So does a good dinner." My belly rumbled and I sure wished the cook would hurry up.

"Patience is a virtue," Mama chided as she plopped a plate and silverware in front of me.

"Sometimes it ain't. I wouldn't call Fripp's patience with Roxbury a virtue. Cheap, more like it."

"True. No one else in town much cottons to Roxbury, either. He ain't welcome at the Tasty Chicken, what with him stealing my cash box and all."

"Or anywhere else in town, either. Wheat's mad at him—so's Thad Ruhl. The old goat poisoned his well good and proper. I hope he don't come back."

"You, me, and anyone else who's had dealings with him."

* * *

I got up with the first rays of light, dressed in my old clothes, and bundled up my new ones. That bath sounded awfully inviting. Sassy waited for me at the door, as if she knew right where we was going.

"You don't get a bath, leastways, not yet. Maybe later." On a hot day, which this promised to be, Sassy did like to splash around in the creek. You'd think she was part otter the way she played in the water.

When I tied the donkey up at the back of the Tasty Chicken, the marshal's horse was gone. That meant I ought not dawdle too long lest he beat me into the office. Why today of all days? A week had gone by since my last bath and I'd really wanted to soak in lavender-scented water until it turned cold. Mama always teased me for liking my baths so much. I'd take one every day if I could.

No one was up so I had to fetch my own water, but I was used to it. The cook had filled the reservoir in the stove before she went to bed, so I didn't have to wait for the water to heat. Mama didn't have no lavender so I settled for rose petals. The bathwater smelled like a flower garden after a rainstorm. I shucked off my clothes and stepped into the tub. The water was so hot that I could only sit a little at a time, but eventually the only thing that stuck out of the water was my face.

Baths—one of life's greatest pleasures. My arms and legs relaxed and I felt free, letting the water do all the work. I lay there and soaked, not fretting about Fripp or Roxbury or Clem Walton. Not haggling in my mind whether I should buy a rifle or a horse first, or whether I should rent a house. All I thought about was how good that water felt and smelled. My little bit of heaven.

When I got my own place, the first thing I'd buy myself would be a big tub just like this one—big enough that all of me would fit in.

Life was good. Sure, old Fripp aggravated the hell out of me, but he was mostly harmless. I'd thought a lot about his entry to Bougie's Saloon, though—that low, bossy voice he used when he took charge made everyone take notice. Might I should practice using a tone that would have that effect.

Roxbury done his best to make life miserable for all of us, but he'd left town, which I was damn glad of. And then I thanked my lucky stars and all beyond that I didn't have to make my living on my back like my mama. What a sorry existence. She didn't ever like servicing men, and now she just headed things up at the Tasty Chicken. The only customer she had was Papa's occasional visits, and I wouldn't exactly call him a customer. Just a few months ago, I reckoned whoring was all I could do.

But this lawdogging business suited me pretty danged good. Steady pay, and not all that much work. In fact, maybe I should thank Roxbury for livening things up a mite.

Marshal Fripp's roar shattered my peace, dang his hide. I stayed put and didn't slosh the water so's I could piece out what he was hollering about. Something about he left his horse and it turned into a donkey. But that didn't make no sense. I heard banging on the walls and shouts from others to shut up. Everyone in the whole damn house had to be awake by now.

My peaceful bath was over before the water even got cool. I hauled my ass out of the tub, dried off, and put on my new duds in a hurry—not how I wanted to end my relaxing time, but so be it. Mostly, I worried about Sassy. Anytime the marshal hollered about a donkey, Sassy was in trouble. I wondered what she done this time.

When I went into the lounge where Fripp and Mama were, the marshal was hitching up his britches and buckling on his gunbelt. Once he saw me, he growled, "Get up a posse. We're going after a horse thief."

"A horse thief? Who?"

"Likely that damned Roxbury, I don't know. Round up five men, and get Wakum. He's a helluva tracker."

I went out the back way and fetched Sassy, then headed to the gunshop. I wasn't real sure what to do if Wakum didn't want to go. He didn't much like Fripp, and he might tell me to piss up a rope. On the way, I ran into Thad Ruhl, who was unlocking his store.

"Marshal Fripp wants me to round up a posse to hunt down a horse thief. Wanna go?"

"Hell no."

"Might be Roxbury."

"I'll get my gunbelt and fetch my horse at the livery."

I was proud of myself for not cracking a smile. "Meet Fripp at the Tasty Chicken and see if you can collect a few more men on the way. I'm on my way to the gunshop."

And then it occurred to me—I couldn't ride with them. The first posse since I became deputy, and I didn't have no horse, nor did I know if I could even stay on one. I vowed right then and there that Fripp wouldn't be leaving me in the dust again.

Chapter 9

Holding Down The Fort

Wakum had just set out his pistol cleaning supplies when I walked in the tent.

"I ain't open yet," he said without looking up.

"Not here to buy nothing, either," I said. "Marshal Fripp is getting up a posse and he wants to make sure you're in it."

"Not interested, especially if it's his idea." Wakum fetched himself a cup of coffee, then held it up, offering me a cup.

"Yeah, I'd like some. Thanks." I had to talk him into riding with Fripp or I'd never hear the end of it. "Says you're the best tracker in these here parts."

"That's a fact."

"Don't you even want to know what the posse is for?"

"Nope."

"Someone stole his horse."

Wakum grinned wide. "No shit!"

"Yep—while he was knockin' boots with Sour Sal at the Tasty Chicken."

"I got work to do here, Honey." He picked up a rag and commenced to polishing the barrel of a Smith and Wesson. "Looking for Fripp's horse is damned low on what'll make me any money."

"Says he thinks Roxbury stole it."

"Roxbury?" Wakum laughed again. "It might be worth it to go just to see how Fripp doesn't arrest that bastard this time."

"You got an extra horse for me?" Sassy chose that particular moment to slobber on the back of my neck.

"Why? Ain't you gonna ride your donkey?"

This wasn't the day to razz me, what with the marshal spoiling my bath and all. I took a swipe and got most of the slobber off my neck. "Do you?"

"Nope. Looks like you'll be holding down the fort here in town while we go chasing after someone with a big head start who knows the hills better than any of us. Ain't looking forward to long, hot days in the saddle for nothing."

"Damn." Not that I'd ridden more than a couple times in my whole life, but how hard could it be to stay perched on top of a horse. "Well, I'll head back over to the whorehouse and tell Fripp you're coming with him."

"No, you tell him he's coming with me."

Me and Sassy took off for the Tasty Chicken. On the way, I made up my mind to ask Wheat to sell me a good horse—better be tame. If I was gonna be a deputy, I wanted to do my job right, and that meant riding in the posse.

Once I met up with the marshal, he was nearly ready to go with a rental horse and a borrowed saddle. Ruhl and a few others stood around, checking their canteens and tie-downs. Not a one of them looked the type that could mix it up with a hard case, but at least the marshal had himself a posse.

"You get Wakum?" Fripp asked.

"Yep. He took some talking to, but he finally agreed. He'll be here shortly—packing up now."

"Go on back to the office, then. Keep the coffee hot."

As if that was all I was good for. Some day this turned out to be. What had started out as a nice rose-smelling soak in the tub had gone to hell in a handbasket. That made me even madder.

But I kept my counsel. "Coffee's always on. Hope it don't take you too long."

"Me, too." He grunted as he pulled himself up into the saddle. Looked to me like he was getting a mite old for chasing outlaws and such. Me and Sassy stood like a couple of stumps watching the posse ride out. Dang it all, I wanted to be with them.

Mama fussed over me some once I got back inside. "Let me braid your hair, Honey. It's a fright."

"Didn't have time to brush it after my bath. It's still wet."

"Well, you just set yourself down in front of the stove, and we'll get you fixed up in no time."

"Nothing fancy, Mama. Just a braid down the back so's my hat fits."

But she had that look and I knew she'd do whatever she damned well pleased. One thing I learned early on—if Mama took a notion to work on my hair, I might as well plant my butt in the chair and let her do it or she'd drive me crazy.

I wouldn't tell her as much, but it was downright enjoyable having her fix my hair. She was good at it, too. But I didn't want no fancy chignon while I was making my rounds.

"I'll just brush it really good for you," she said. "Then I'll make a braid just like you asked." She brushed the ends and worked up. "Your hair's the same color as your pa's used to be. So pretty—that light brown with just a hint of red. I learned right off not to call it 'strawberry blond.' It's about time he showed up in town."

I knew very well what color Papa's hair was, but Mama liked talking about him so I let her rattle on. But he'd likely take exception to her description. My pa wasn't exactly what I'd call pretty. He was handsome, all right, but there was a big difference between handsome and pretty. She seemed a mite wistful so I didn't go on about it.

"Papa's starting to get gray around the temples."

"And losing a little up top." Mama chuckled in that way that showed how fond she was of him. "But he's still the handsomest man I ever did see."

"He sure wouldn't let a posse ride off without him." I had enough mad stored up to last me a while.

"No, he'd have been on the trail before they'd manage to get one together. He don't fool around, that one." She put down the brush and separated my hair into three hanks for braiding. "I have a nice ribbon to tie it off with."

"Mama, I can't be wearing ribbons and act like a lawdog."

"There's nothing weak about being womanly, Honey. We bear the children, and we bear the burden of men's needs. A weakling wouldn't hold up, and neither would a man. If you don't believe me, then let me know how you think a man would deal with bleeding once a month, or pushing out a young'un. So I ain't impressed with your deputying, at least, not that it's a tougher job than what my girls do, because it ain't."

"You're right, Mama. I don't ever forget it, either. I was thinking about that very thing before Fripp put the kibosh on my nice bath, and even though he's an ass, I'm thankful you made him hire me."

* * *

I walked back to the livery to take my old clothes back, and also had a faint hope that Sassy might stay there and visit with her friends. But the main reason was I wanted to talk to Wheat about buying a horse.

"Not a one that would suit you," Wheat said. He was pitching hay to some mares. "I'll keep an eye out for one, though."

"The sooner, the better. How much do they run?"

"A good one will cost you better than a hundred dollars."

A hundred dollars? I tried not to let him know I was plumb flabbergasted. "I ain't got that much."

"I know. Might give you credit."

"I'll think on it once you find a horse that'd do me."

With that, I headed to the marshal's office, Sassy dogging me every step. Once we got there, she brayed at me on account of I wouldn't let her come in.

"You don't wipe your hooves and you ain't housetrained, so just entertain yourself outside." I shut the door and the next thing I knew, that danged donkey was looking at me through the window. She had a forlorn look and I was tempted to let her in, but a marshal's office wasn't a livery and she didn't belong in there.

Sometimes I wondered if I belonged, but I'd do my double damnedest to make it work out. I made up my mind to take her back to the livery at noon—maybe she'd stay. Worth a try.

The stack of paperwork Fripp left for me wasn't going anywhere so I dove in. The ledger work bored me to tears but it had to be done, especially since the marshal pinched every penny. Of course, Mama ended up with a goodly share of those pennies, which made his cheap-ass ways a lot less aggravating. Dr. George hadn't brought his bill in yet, though, and Fripp would likely take some of my pay to cover it since I pulled the trigger.

After an hour or so of that, I stood and stretched, then went to get some coffee. But only a lump of grounds plopped into my cup. I took the bucket and went outside to fetch some water. Of course, Sassy stuck her nose in it first thing.

"You are the most obnoxious donkey I've ever seen." I rubbed her ears and then her neck and back. The lash marks had all healed up real fine thanks to Wheat's liniment. It stunk to high hell, but it did the trick.

"Get that stupid donkey away from the front of the hotel!" the clerk called.

I reckoned he thought someone might confuse Sassy for him, as ugly as he was, and he didn't want that. But I had no truck with him. "Don't you worry yourself none. I've got my water and we're on our way." I patted Sassy on the butt. So Fripp's coffee would have a little donkey spit in it. "C'mon, girl. We ain't wanted here."

I hadn't taken a step before I heard a fellow hollering.

"Ha!" The man's voice was vaguely familiar. "There she is—the whore-deputy."

Coming at me was none other than Clem Piss-Poor-

Shot Walton and his two brothers, one on each side of him. Actually, he wasn't that bad of a shot, but he didn't smell much better than Wheat's liniment, and the smell was the best part of Clem.

"You've got me for the night, Honey Beaulieu." He wobbled some, the whiskey showing none too kindly on his demeanor, but his holster and pistol was poised, ready for a quick cross-draw. "I bet you wanna be on top."

On top of his grave, maybe. "Go sleep it off, Walton." I hoped he'd be drunk enough to take a snooze right there, but no such luck. What was worse, neither of his brothers looked like they'd been drinking with him, because they walked straight—glared straight, too. Just my luck that they were stone sober. All three were well-heeled.

"Thought that you, Miss Uppity Britches, might wanna see how good you can shoot when someone's shooting back." Clem laughed at his own saying. No one else did.

"You thought wrong." I had one six-gun bein's no trouble afoot, and it held five rounds. There was only three of them—a brother on each side of Clem—and they was lots bigger targets than bottles. Closer, too. My rapid fire was decent, but if they could handle a shootin' iron at all, one of them would get me. Clem could hit bottles well enough, but I had no idea how good the other two was.

"We'll see about that. Come to my room and show me what all you learned at the Tasty Chicken."

"I can tell you that right now. I learned to stay away from scalawags the likes of you."

He shrugged, and dang near tipped over. "In that case, I think we should have us another shooting match right here, right now."

Clem pulled, quicker than I'd given him credit for, and shot through the upstairs hotel window. Glass shattered and a woman screamed. With luck, the shot only scared her, and didn't hurt her. At least if she was screaming, she wasn't dead.

I stood my ground, even though my legs told me that was not a smart thing to do. They wanted to head for the nearest cover. Thing of it was, Sassy could get hit, and my best option was to make sure they didn't cut loose no other bullets.

"Get along, Sassy." I smacked her on the rump good. "Get back to the livery." Miracle of all miracles, she actually went. Now I could get down to business.

"I think I just might see if I can shoot her ears off. Wouldn't that be a sight—a donkey with no ears?" He laughed again as Sassy trotted by him, pulling his pistol and sighting in on her. His brothers stood stern-faced, not laughing with him.

I wanted to plug the bastard right in the forehead, but the difference between him and me was just that—he did what he wanted without worrying about harming others. Even threatened, I'd be damned if I'd ever be such a snake. But Clem made hanging onto my temper a sore trial.

"You do that and you're under arrest."

"Well now, we all know Fripp didn't give you permission to arrest me, let alone my brothers, so we won't be visiting your jail." By then, Sassy had trotted on down the road toward the livery.

Both Clem's brothers took a step away from him to make it harder for me to hit all three. I studied each for a tell. Clem would give me plenty of warning, what with him so drunk. The nervous brother's shoulder would likely stop twitching once he decided to pull. But I couldn't put a make on the third.

"Pull as you hit the dirt and take out Budge first. He's the brother on the right."

There was that man's voice again. Wished I could figure out who in tarnation was doggin' me. Or maybe I was losing my marbles. Whatever, I needed to keep my focus on stinky Clem and his ornery brothers if I wanted to get out of this without being shot full of holes.

Chapter 10

A Deputy With No Horse?

Clem looked the maddest of the three obnoxious men standing in the street, waiting for my next move. I reckoned he could blow anytime and I was ready, but I worried for Sassy who might decide she didn't want to go to the livery after all.

The Walton brother on the left looked nervous—his shoulder twitched, and his hand inched toward the grip of his pistol. The Walton brother on Clem's right stood somewhat akimbo, the only one of the three who wasn't tense as a lightning rod.

"He looks relaxed, but he's the quickest."

There was that voice again, dang it all. "Who the hell are you?" Damn it all, I knew I shouldn't have said that out loud.

"Never you mind me. Just pay attention, and fire at Budge first."

"Why, we're the Walton brothers," Clem said. "The ones that are fixin' to have a little fun with you."

I started to say I wasn't talking to him, but shut my yap. It was dreadful bad when you start thinking things and then answering yourself. After I shook off the nonsense, I said, "The three of you need to get on home and sleep it off."

"Not before you collect your win. You get me for the

night, remember?"

"The only way I want you for the night is gone." My left hand was ready to pull. "I want you to listen up, 'cause I ain't saying it again. Get out of town now—all three of you."

Mrs. Tench, the mayor's wife, took that moment to cross the street right square between me and the Waltons. How she couldn't see the obnoxious turds, nor hear all the hollering and the gunshot, was beyond me. Clem grabbed her around the neck and she squeaked, likely on account of her tight corset wouldn't let her scream. He prodded her temple with his pistol.

"Now, Mrs. Tench, I want you to tell Honey to come with me, and there won't be no more trouble."

I couldn't do much but stand there like a moron. If I shot him, he might pull the trigger and blow her brains out. But then she slumped down, catching him unawares, and stabbed him in the cojones with her umbrella. He doubled over. Budge pulled—I drew and shot his pistol hand, then in one motion, cocked and took out the other brother's leg. I meant to shoot his hand, too, but I missed.

Mrs. Tench ran to the boardwalk and hid behind the pickle barrel in front of the Golden Ruhl. That woman earned my respect, but I didn't have time to dwell on it now, for as soon as Clem caught his breath, he'd be shooting at me. I ran toward him and using all the force I could, kicked him in the jaw with my brand-new boots. That laid him out, but then his brother—the one with the wounded leg—found his six-gun in the dirt a few feet away and reached for it.

"You touch that and Doc's gonna have to patch up

your hand besides your leg."

He slumped back and rested like a good boy. The first one, Budge, snaked his left hand toward his boot. My guess was he had a knife in there.

"Keep your hands up or you're a dead man."

That stopped him cold. Unfortunately, I didn't have handcuffs nor any rope to tie these bounders up with, so they'd just have to walk.

"Budge, Clem, help your brother up. We're going to Doc's." I cocked my Peacemaker so they knew I meant business.

"My arm's busted," Budge whined.

"No, it ain't—your hand's busted. Now help your brother."

Clem clawed his way to his knees. "I'm gonna puke."

Can't say as I much felt sorry for him. "Go right on ahead. Then help Budge with your brother."

Mrs. Tench stood and stepped out from behind the pickle barrel as she straightened her bonnet, then called inside the store for help. I couldn't quite hear what she said but a few customers ran to her side. She whisked them my direction, then stuck her nose in the air and marched off as if not a danged thing had happened. I couldn't help but think we should all salute her. The mayor could take a lesson.

When the helpers got to me, I said, "Help the one with the hurt leg. The other two are just feeling puny—make sure they keep moving."

They helped me get the two wounded Waltons to the doctor's office. I locked Clem in the outhouse back of the jail, since I couldn't arrest him without Fripp's permission.

"You can't leave me in here!" he hollered.

"I can't?" And I walked off, headed to the livery to check on Sassy.

* * *

Wheat had ridden with the posse so a man who worked for him on occasion, Nolan Radison, greeted me at the door with a pitchfork of hay and Sassy nibbling on his ear. "This your beast?"

"I bought her, and she let me, if that's what you mean."

"Been pestering me for half an hour."

"She's been pestering me for two weeks, and I expect it won't end anytime soon."

"Got a john in today—racing mule. Not sure if Wheat's gonna want to keep him on account of no one can ride him. Leastways, that's what the sporting man said when he left him here."

"Left him?"

"Yep. The gambler had some men after him and he was in what you might call a rush. I expect he didn't play square. Anyway, he ran in here, took his horse and rode out bareback—left his fancy saddle, too. Said Wheat could have the mule for payment—but the bill only came to a buck and two bits. Even an ornery mule is worth fifty."

"Racing mule, you say?"

"Yep. Good size and well fed. Good hooves and teeth. Wouldn't mind having a mule like that myself if he was ridable."

"How do you know he ain't?"

"Bucked when I tried to mount him. That ain't a good sign."

No, but it might mean the mule would be cheaper than a horse.

"And another thing. That danged donkey of yours made friends with this mule right off. The mule calmed down considerable once the jenny showed up."

"Think I oughta talk to Wheat about buying this mule?"

"Not if you want to keep your teeth where they're supposed to be."

Hell, I didn't even know how to ride. Even thinking about buying such an obnoxious animal was pure-dee folly.

"Think I'll go get something to eat. Want I should bring you something?"

"Naw, the wife will be here pretty soon—likely have enough for you if you have a notion to stick around."

"I best get back to the office. I locked Clem Walton in the outhouse and he's not happy about it."

Sassy came running along once she saw me walk out of the livery. What a pesky critter! She nosed into my vest pocket looking for a treat, and I gave her the last bit of my peppermint stick. The clock bell struck noon right about the time my stomach growled, and I headed to Tex's Café. I had a hankerin' for some of Mrs. Adams's peach pie and no one made it good as she did.

Some things in life were a trial that ought not be. One of those was walking into a restaurant and convincing Sassy to stay outside. I tied her to the hitching rail, but she untied the rope as fast as I could knot it.

"You have to stay out here, you ornery donkey. I'll get my food and come outside to visit with you while I eat it—but you can't have my peach pie."

I swear, that donkey whined, but at least she didn't follow me inside that time. And just for insurance, I bought two pieces of peach pie.

"I'll be eating on the boardwalk, but I'll bring the dishes back in. You don't have to worry none."

"They best not be broken," Mrs. Adams said, "else I'll send Tex after your sorry hide, and that donkey's, too."

Truth of it was, most folks was more scared of her than Tex. Including Tex.

"I'll be careful, ma'am."

"So you didn't ride with the posse, eh?"

"No horse."

The town's best baker raised her eyebrow. "A deputy with no horse?"

"Never had a need of one before."

One of the fellows at the counter who'd just been served a big piece of custard pie slapped me on the back. "A posse's no place for a woman. You're best off right here in town."

Mrs. Adams snatched his plate away. "Tell that to Clem Walton and his useless brothers."

"Hey, I wasn't done with that pie yet."

She shoved it back in front of him. "Watch your mouth in my restaurant."

He held onto the saucer and took a bite before she swiped it again. "But no deputy can do a full job without a horse."

"You're right about that." Mrs. Adams brought my food. "Want me to help you carry it outside?"

As we passed by, I saw several men sneak glances at me and heard murmurs of "She don't even have a horse!"

It was getting mighty old, I don't mind saying.

First people thought a woman couldn't be a deputy and now they put it out that a deputy with no horse was no deputy at all. At least I had a donkey.

I sat on the boardwalk but before my butt hit the wood, Sassy scarfed up both pieces of peach pie.

* * *

After Doc George patched up the two Walton brothers, I tied them up and sent a message to their mama to fetch them. She drove her farm wagon into town a few hours later.

"That's two—where's Clem?" She was a sturdy woman not given to chatter.

"In the outhouse behind the marshal's office." I motioned for her to follow me.

"Why didn't you throw him in jail?" She clambered onto the wagon and took up the lines. Mrs. Walton released the brake. "Get on, now," she said as she snapped the lines.

"Fripp don't want to feed the prisoners. Clem's gonna be a mite peckish once I open the door."

"When I get that boy home, he's gonna get the what-for—getting his brothers all shot up and such on account of him thinking with his pecker, if he was thinking at all. Ain't no call for that."

Much as I loathed Clem and his brothers, I took a liking to their mama right then and there. "I'll buy you a cup of coffee at Tex's Café before you leave town, if you take a notion."

"D'ruther have a little nip of whiskey."

"Bougie's Saloon, then."

"I have supplies to buy and some boys to hug right after I smack the daylights out of them. How about I meet you there when I come to town next Saturday?"

I nodded, then me and Sassy cut across between the marshal's office and the next building that housed the mayor's office while Mrs. Walton drove her wagon around the block.

By the time she got there, I'd already commenced to untying the rope I'd used to keep the door shut. "He's in here." Clem had finally stopped pounding and hollering. I hoped he hadn't passed out or some such. "Your mama's here," I said, a bit louder than normal in case he might be taking a snooze. "I'm letting you out now." The knot was stubborn but I finally got it untied.

I stepped back and Mrs. Walton opened the door. Clem sat there with his chin propped on his hands.

"I don't feel so good, Ma."

Chapter 11

Hankering For A Poker Game

Clem Walton sat in the one-holer, his elbows on his knees and his britches around his ankles. He did look a mite on the green side—whether from being roostered, or smelling the outhouse fumes, it was anyone's guess. Likely both. Either way, I didn't much care.

Neither did his mama. Mrs. Walton grabbed him by the shirtsleeve and gave him a tug. "You get in the wagon with your brothers and you stay put. I got errands to do in town." She dragged him to the wagon, then gave him a swat on the butt as he climbed onto the bed. "Until then, stay set, and shut up. You hear me, boy?"

"Yes, Ma."

"Once we get home, we'll have us a little chat. I ain't exactly happy with the lot of you." She clambered into the driver's seat and they all headed to the Golden Ruhl.

I reckoned the Walton brothers were in good hands so I took off for the marshal's office and commenced to shuffling more papers. Can't say as if paperwork was my favorite thing, but it beat the hell out of getting shot at. Which actually was the paperwork—I had to write up a report about how them Walton boys ended up full of holes. That alone took me half an hour.

Thad Ruhl brought in the mail—no new wanted posters but the U.S. marshal did send a list of bounties that had already been claimed, so I went through my stack of posters and threw out all the ones listed. That got rid of several, but even more waited to be collected. If a man brought in all the bounties left, I calculated he'd be close to ten thousand dollars richer.

"Damn, that's a lot of money," I muttered. Quite a few of the hard cases had bounties of five hundred dollars or more on them. Some of them had been on the loose for a couple years—money on the hoof.

At noon I locked up, intending to fetch some grub for me and Sassy. The finest place in town to eat was the Tasty Chicken, so that's where I was headed, because it was also the best place to hear all the latest goings on. The patrons of the Tasty Chicken would know any news about the posse before anyone else in town, on account of the posse would likely stop there first.

Besides, I had a hankering for a poker game. Since the day Fripp hired me, I'd stayed away from the game, but just in case Mama needed a dealer, I could help out for an hour or so. Sassy nudged my back to hurry me along. She knew Mama would have some good vittles for her, too.

"Maybe I should teach you how to deal. Wouldn't that be something." But then that blasted donkey pulled my shirt and wanted me to go to the livery, which surprised me because she liked hanging around the Tasty Chicken. The girls there paid her special attention, and she ate that up like molasses. "You go on, then. Meet me back at the marshal's office."

Sassy trotted away, swishing her tail. Now whether she'd have enough sense to meet me later was up to chance, but then I was in a gambling mood anyway.

The familiar smell of cigar smoke and whiskey combined with roast beef, fried chicken, and gravy greeted me when I walked into the Tasty Chicken. So did Mama, who gave me a big ol' bear hug.

"I see you came just in time to eat."

"Thought you might need a dealer for an hour, too."

"That I do." Mama turned to the bartender. "Hank, clear off the corner table. Honey's scaring up a poker game." She went to the window and flipped over the poker sign so men walking by would know this was the place where they could find a good game. "You have plenty of time to eat before we get enough players so sit down and I'll have Cook bring you something."

Growing up in a whorehouse isn't the best place for a kid. A whore's daughter had to stay out of the way during working hours, and during the day the girls in school treated me like chicken shit. But I learned things they'd never even dream of—for instance, I could stock a deck by the time I was ten, and was pretty decent at three-card monte, too.

Life in a whorehouse did have its good points, such as I always had a comfortable bed and a great bath. But the best advantage was good food. Mama always said the girls couldn't work hard if they weren't fed and happy, and besides, she could charge more for the whores who had a little meat on their bones.

Customers kept wanting to eat and oftentimes came in right after work, so Mama had finally caved in and expanded the Tasty Chicken to include a restaurant—the best dang restaurant in town. Of course, she'd always had a saloon and a gambling room to keep the gentlemen busy while they waited for a turn upstairs. She was proud of the fact that the Tasty Chicken provided the best whiskey, whores, and food in the territory.

And the best poker, too. "Maybe I should scare up a game tomorrow instead. Some of the regular players rode out with the posse."

Mama shrugged. "There's plenty still in town. If you come in later this afternoon, there'll be train passengers here who are staying overnight."

"Not sure I'll be able to make it in later."

By the time I finished my roast beef dinner, four players had showed up—no surprise, the banker came in first. After a few minutes, the carpenter and his friend happened by, and then the brewer joined us.

"I brought you a few barrels and saw the poker sign. Might sit in for a few hands." He drew a mug from one of the barrels and offered it to me.

"No thanks. I'm not much on strong drink during the day." Especially when dealing. I always play square unless someone's trying to pull a fast one, then I might deal seconds. Even then, I've never resorted to lizards or mirrors like some do, although I know how to use them. "Be seated, fellows. I only have an hour so it'll be a quick game, but maybe Mama will have time to take over once I get back to work."

I lost a few games and won a few. By the end of my hour, I was ahead fifty bucks and two barrels of beer for the Tasty Chicken. I stashed the money in Mama's strong box—she'd split it up with me later—and visited with the girls for a few minutes.

On the way out, I heard whimpering that sounded like

it was coming from the storeroom, so instead of leaving, I turned around and headed to see what the problem was. Usually, one of the girls had a broken heart—some customer would make big promises of marrying her and then never show up again.

This time, I didn't recognize the gal who was huddled behind one of the new beer barrels, and she wasn't dressed like a whore, neither, what with her modest calico dress and sunbonnet. I squatted beside her and patted her back.

"Can I help you with something, miss?"

Tears streamed down her cheeks. She rubbed at her eyes and sniffed. I think she started to say something but only a whimper came out.

"Ah, it can't be as bad as all that. I'm Honey Beaulieu. My mama owns the Tasty Chicken and I'm the deputy here at Fry Pan Gulch. You got a name?"

She took a deep breath and said, "Em—Em—Emma."

"You from around here?"

Emma shook her head and pointed over her shoulder, but where she pointed was to the center of town, so that didn't make no sense.

"Maybe from a ranch outside of town?"

She nodded.

"Tell me what you're crying about, Emma. Maybe I can help."

After a moment, she shook her head. "No one can help me." Her words was more of a squeak.

"Well, you wouldn't be here if you didn't think someone could."

"Guess I hope to work here."

Now I knew she was in trouble, on account of no little

gal like her would come within fifty feet of the Tasty Chicken if she didn't have to. "I don't think you want to work here. Maybe I can see if there's a job at the store or the boardinghouse. You can cook and clean?"

"They won't want me." Then the waterworks started all over again.

"Emma, you're gonna have to tell me the whole story or I can't do a thing for you. Best you start at the beginning." I pulled a hankie out of my pocket and handed it to her.

"Well, there's this handsome man—he lives on the next ranch over—and he came courting."

"That don't sound so bad."

"And we got along good. I was tickled that he'd even notice me, bein's I'm on the plain side and all."

Emma didn't look plain to me. Sometimes folks, especially women, had odd notions about how they really look. She had pretty brown hair and big blue eyes. Looked like she had a nice shape, too—nothing anyone but her would call plain. Maybe her old blue calico dress was plain, but not her.

"You're a nice-looking gal, Emma, so just let that part rest. Now go on with your story."

"Well, he wanted to kiss me and such. I let him and it was nice. Really nice."

Uh oh. I knew where this was going, and I decided to save her the trouble of saying it. "So he said if you loved him, you'd let him do what married folks do. Right?"

She nodded.

"And now there's a bun in the oven?" Judging by the new onslaught of tears, I'd made the right call. "I'm taking you to Mama and see if she'll let you stay in my old room until we figure out what you need to do. Don't worry, it ain't a working room—just a room. Have you seen Dr. George yet?" I took her arm and pulled her to her feet.

"No, ma'am."

"Just call me Honey. C'mon and we'll get you fixed up for the time bein'."

I still had a key so I took her to my room first, then went to fetch Mama. "There's a girl named Emma in my room—nice girl. Some ranch hand knocked her up and she's crying buckets. She's in a bad way. Think you could go talk to her?"

"I will, but you know I don't have a damned thing to offer her that would help much. You say she ain't a whore—you know I don't like to take green girls. Let someone else ruin them. Can't bring myself to do it even though it's good business."

"Maybe not, but she could use a little understanding right about now. You can give her my share of the poker money and she can rent my room for a week—I'm hardly ever here since I moved to the livery."

"Which I still don't know why you did. There's not a blasted thing wrong with your room and men know not to bother you there."

"And I appreciate that, Mama. I really do. It's just time for me to make my own way and you know it, or you'd never have hounded Fripp into giving me a job in the first place."

She gave me a hug. "I'm downright proud of you, Honey. Your girl can stay in the room—I'll even send food up to her if she don't feel like coming down. But you need to figure out what to do with her because this ain't no place for a girl like her and you know it."

"Well, it's *some* place, and it's better than her hiding out in the storeroom or on the street where's she's liable to run into a whole lot worse trouble."

"True. Now, take me up to your room and introduce us."

Chapter 12

This Coffee Tastes Like Cow Piss

Turned out, that handsome ranch hand was Clem Walton, the one and the same who slept off his drunk in the outhouse. Why Emma thought he was worth her respectability, I have no idea. Women didn't seem to have much sense when it came to men.

But none of that mattered at this point. What she needed was a place to live where she could raise her baby—and hope to blazes it don't turn out like him. Or look like him, either.

Sassy had stayed at the livery all during my poker break and met me when I walked out of the Tasty Chicken. We headed to the marshal's office. When we got there, a fellow was sleeping on the bench beside the door—and I recognized the horse tied to the hitching rail. Yup, it was my pa.

He eyed me up and down and then gave me a big hug. Once he was done squeezing the stuffing out of me, he set me back at arm's length and gave me another looking over. "Why are you wearing britches, Honey, and what's the story on that badge you have pinned to your vest?"

"I'm deputy here at Fry Pan now."

"Where's Fripp?"

"Posse. A fellow named Roxbury stole his horse."

"Roxbury? That sonofabitch has a bounty on him.

Fraud. Goes by Ed Berry. When he hits a new town, he tells folks he found color and then he sells them a passel of worthless claims."

"He didn't do that here, although he made a pest of himself plenty enough, that sticky-fingered old rascal. You got business in town?"

Papa motioned to a horse standing beside his that carried a man who was tied and gagged. "Need to store this here owlhoot in your jail while I collect the bounty."

"How much?"

"He's only worth a hundred dollars. Cost me half that to track him down, but it was a close job and I ain't getting any younger."

Sure seemed like a lot of money to me. I unlocked the door to the office. "Let me get a cell ready and then you can bring him in."

By the time I was ready for him, Papa had his prisoner waiting at the door and we locked him up. I was hoping Papa would stay in town for a while so I asked him what was coming up next.

"After this, I'll supply up and go fetch the Palomino Kid. A thousand-dollar bounty."

"I seen his poster." Damn, that seemed like a big pile of money. I put some coffee on to boil. "You staying in town long?"

"Nope. Plan to see Agnes, take care of business, and get on the train."

Pa looked like he could use a snort so I got the whiskey bottle out of the desk drawer and poured him a good belt—three fingers. Then, for the pure-dee hell of it, I poured a splash in my own glass—not much, just enough to wet my whistle.

He took one big gulp and tossed back his head while the liquor trickled down his throat. "So how'd you end up Fripp's deputy? He ain't none too ambitious."

"Not unless he's at the Tasty Chicken. The girls tell me he can get downright rambunctious at times." Papa wandered about the office looking at this and that. He picked up my vase of posies and studied on it for a bit, then put it back down on the desk. "Ain't never seen this place so clean. Must be your doing."

"Yep. Fripp thinks I'm his maid." Which reminded me—I didn't have the marshal's permission to jail Pa's prisoner. "And I can't arrest no one. He's gonna be pissed what with you bringing a prisoner here on account of the meals come out of his budget."

"Sounds like something he'd say."

"So because of that, on one dustup I just shot them rowdies. Of course, Fripp got mad because he had to pay Doc, so there's no winning this game. The last fracas was with the Walton brothers. I sent two of them to Doc and locked one in the outhouse until his mama fetched him."

Which reminded me of Emma and her unborn baby. She could sure use five hundred or a thousand dollars to get situated before the baby's due date.

Papa put his hat on. "I best go see Agnes now. You coming over to the Tasty Chicken later?"

Agnes was my mama and she'd be tickled to peppermint sticks to see my pa. "Be there at about six. That's just in time for supper."

Sassy chose that moment to bray through the door, then come in. It hadn't taken her long to learn how to turn the knob.

“You keeping livestock in here now?” Papa asked.

“Naw, that there’s just my donkey. I bought her from Roxbury, er, Berry.”

Once I told him the story, he chuckled. “You always was too soft-hearted for your own good.”

* * *

The posse came back empty handed. I seen them riding in midafternoon kicking up enough dust to be noticed a mile away. I dashed into the office and put on a fresh pot of coffee on account of Fripp would need to be buttered up once he found out he had to feed a prisoner. I reckoned Pa could explain that to him—no need for me to.

Roxbury kept dogging my thoughts, damn his hide. I’d go fetch him myself but I didn’t have no horse. Besides, I had a job to do right here in Fry Pan Gulch. A hundred dollars was a lot of money but Emma would need more than that. Of course, Emma wasn’t none of my concern.

Wheat had stayed at the livery so only Fripp, Wakum, and Ruhl came to the marshal’s office. Fripp dismounted as did the general store owner, but Wakum tipped his hat to me then took the reins of the other two men’s horses and led them toward the livery. Sassy trotted along behind and nipped his ear, then came back.

Ruhl hitched up his britches. “We could’ve used you out there, Honey. Too bad you ain’t got a horse.” He laughed and I went into the office, much as I hated to be around Fripp when he was in a bad mood, which I knew he would be. Roxbury was gone and so was the marshal’s horse. Fripp wasn’t none too happy about either, or buying food for Pa's prisoner, and he took it out on me.

"This coffee tastes like cow piss."

"I must be improving then."

"If you was worth your salt, you'd have gone with the posse."

Damn. He had a point there. I made up my mind to get me a mount—only problem was, I didn't have enough money.

"And get that damned donkey out of here."

"We're heading to the livery now."

"Hobble the blasted beast. Just keep her where she belongs—and she don't belong here."

Not a way in the world was I about to hobble Sassy, but I sure was tempted to hobble Fripp's mouth.

* * *

That evening, I went to the Tasty Chicken to have supper with Papa and Mama. They was already at the table, so Pa stood and hugged me, then seated me.

"Did you wash up proper?" Mama asked.

"Yes I did, for I knew you'd holler at me if I didn't."

Pa chuckled. "I've been poking around. Seems like you've made quite an impression as a lawdog, Honey."

"Just holding my own, mostly."

"Agnes tells me you won a shooting match."

"Eh. Not much competition—a big-headed fool. Turns out he also knocked up a sweet little gal. Mama's letting her stay in my room for the time being."

"Where are you living, then?"

"Wheat rented me a loft room at the livery. I ain't got it fixed up yet, but you're welcome to come visit."

Mama patted Papa on the leg. "How long are you

staying, Devlin?" Mama was the only one who called him by his first name. Everyone else called him Beaulieu, or if they couldn't get all that off their tongue, then Blue. I doubted most folks even knew his first name, and that suited Pa just fine.

"Leaving day after tomorrow on the morning train."

He'd be in town a whole day! "How about we go shooting tomorrow?"

"Might have time after I buy supplies and take care of business." We all knew part of that business would be with Mama. She smiled at him and I grinned at her.

Even though Papa and Mama never married and weren't even together all that much, I treasured times like this here supper. Sorta made me feel part of a real family.

"I hear tell you didn't ride with the posse because you don't have a horse." He held up his cup and one of the gals brought the coffee pot.

When she'd filled all our cups and left, I said, "That, and Fripp didn't ask me." Fripp never did much cotton to Pa, likely because Pa was taller, better looking, and a much better shot. The marshal only tolerated me on account of I did all his work for him.

"He might be worried about you poaching his headlines."

"That ain't gonna happen. I get too danged much attention as it is."

"I expect so, you being a girl and all." He turned to Mama. "What you got in mind for supper?"

"Roast beef, potatoes and gravy, apple pie, and a whiskey chaser."

He grinned. "My favorite."

"I thought I was your favorite."

"Next favorite, then."

Well, hey, I was sitting there, too. "What about me? Am I number three?"

"Honey, ain't no doubt about it—you're one of a kind."

* * *

It had been a long couple days for me and they wasn't done yet, for Fripp went home early and left me with the charge of the prisoner, and I got strict orders not to feed him too much. If Wakum hadn't volunteered for a few hours of duty, I couldn't have joined Papa and Mama for supper.

Oh sure, I could've made Pa sit watch, but Mama didn't get to be with him much and I hated to take what little time she did have away from her. But dang Wakum for being so obliging on account of now I felt guilty for not buying that rifle from him.

"You thought about that rifle, Honey?" Wakum said as I walked into the marshal's office.

"It's a beaut, all right. But it seems like every time I get ten dollars, there's a hundred dollars more of stuff to buy."

"Welcome to the world of living on your own. It's a jolt when you first fly out of the nest."

"I can't decide what to buy first. The posse left me in the dust because I don't have a horse. But even if I did, it'd need a saddle and bridle which I don't have. And when you ride with a posse, you need a rifle, which I don't have, or the cartridges for it. Then there's the war bag and all that goes in it. That don't even count fixing up my room in the livery, or helping that girl."

"What girl?"

"Emma—she didn't say her last name. Clem Walton knocked her up and she's staying in my room at the Tasty Chicken for the time being."

"Is he gonna marry her?"

"I hope to blazes not. He done bad enough by her already."

Wakum left and I fed the prisoner some soup and coffee, then after sending Sassy to the livery—and she actually went—I bedded down in the cell next to his for the night. The prisoner didn't give me no problems. Likely why he was only worth a hundred dollars.

I just about got to sleep when I heard the awfullest clatter outdoors. I still had my clothes on so I pulled on my boots and grabbed a rifle from the gun rack on the way out.

Sassy greeted me. She brought her friend, the racing mule.

Well, crap. What was I gonna do with a donkey and a mule, too?

Chapter 13

You're Fired

Bright and early the next morning, I left the marshal's office and went to the livery. Sassy and her new best friend followed me. There didn't seem to be any question but what she thought that danged mule should be mine. He was tall, nigh onto sixteen hands, and sleek, bein's a thoroughbred mare threw him.

Wheat had already done more work than six normal men by the time I got there, and it wasn't even eight o'clock yet. At the moment, he was shoeing a draft horse.

"Morning, Wheat."

He grunted but didn't look up, for he was heating the horseshoe in the fire.

"I decided you ought to sell me the mule. Sassy and him came to visit me at the jail to deliver the news. So how much?"

Wheat scowled at me and commenced to plinking on the hot horseshoe. "I ain't gonna sell you that mule, Honey."

Sassy and the mule came closer, although neither one of them cottoned to the sound of the bellows, and both shied from the fire.

"What else are you gonna do with that mule, then?"

"Haven't decided. Might sell him to the Indians—they like mule meat."

"Looks like an awful good mule to waste on butchering. Besides, I can't afford a horse. Sell me that blasted mule and at least I'll have something to ride."

"Do you even know how?"

"Well... I reckon me and him will learn together."

"Ain't gonna sell him to you, Honey. That damned mule bucked me off, and Nolan ate dirt, too. What makes you think you can ride him?"

That was a good question, but I knew that me and the mule would make a team. "How about you let me worry about that? Just sell him to me."

"Can't do it and still sleep at night."

"That critter has taken to following me around. Want me to get arrested for mule thieving?"

"Won't happen. Fripp wouldn't want to pay for your food. Besides, he'd have to make his own coffee."

"Aw c'mon, Wheat. I need a mount and it might as well be the mule. Looks like he can run fast as the wind."

"Once he sets his mind to it—and that ain't necessarily when you set your mind to it."

"You think on it, Wheat. I have to fetch my Peacemakers—Papa's taking me shooting today. We can talk about the mule when I get back."

Sure enough, when I climbed down the ladder with my pistols and cartridges, Sassy and the mule were waiting for me. "C'mon, you two rascals. Pa's waiting."

The three of us headed back to the marshal's office, where Pa said he'd be haggling with Fripp for bounty money. Fripp always wanted a cut for storing the prisoner. "If that money went toward jail upkeep, I wouldn't mind paying up," Pa had told me earlier. "But it goes smack dab into Fripp's pocket."

I had reminded him that dang neart any money that Fripp got his hands on eventually ended up in the Tasty Chicken's coffers, but Papa was still in a sour mood.

Sure enough, Pa and Fripp were hollering toe to toe, nose to nose. While they was blowing bad breath all over one another, I went to my desk and did the paperwork, which only took me a few minutes.

"Here's your paperwork." I handed Pa the document. "It might take a few days for the bank to get the money in."

Fripp whirled my direction. "Damn it all, Honey. You can't do that!"

"I just did." I headed toward the door. "Let's go, Papa."

"Then you're fired," Fripp yelled.

I unpinned my badge and threw it to him. He caught it—the pin stuck right square in the middle of his palm. Sorta made me feel good.

But as soon as I stepped on the boardwalk, my spirits took a dive. "Now what the hell am I gonna do for a living?"

Papa chuckled. "I expect the same as always. Once Fripp drinks his own coffee, he'll be wanting you back. Besides, he hates paperwork."

"I don't much like it myself, but at least I get through it once a week. I doubt the marshal did a thing since the day they swore him in unless someone had a gun to his head."

"Yep. Had to stand him down a time or three myself. Usually, I just take prisoners elsewhere, but I like seeing my baby daughter every now and again."

"I ain't much of a baby." But a body couldn't be

prouder standing beside my pa. He was taller than most men and anyone could tell not to mess with him. Women twittered as they went by but he paid them no mind. Men treated him like the lead wolf—wanting him to notice them but taking care not to rile him.

"You'll always be my baby girl, Honey." He gave me a quick side hug. "Let's go bust some bottles."

"I got all day." No job, no income. Damn. Sassy chose that moment to walk up and give me a kiss. The mule acted like he was about to do the same but considering his size, I put my hand out and stopped him. "Don't you go running me over. I ain't even bought you yet."

"You gonna?"

"Wheat says he won't sell him on account of no one can ride him."

"Good for Wheat."

"But I'll talk him into it. The mule's gentle enough. I expect it won't take much to get him saddle broke."

Pa started walking toward Wakum's gunshop and I kept pace with his long strides, the donkey and the mule trailing. Every once in a while, one of them would nose off my hat. "Bunch of pests," I muttered, picking up my hat for about the tenth time.

"Tell you what," he said as we neared the gunshop. "Next time I'm around—likely in another couple months—I'll buy you a horse. Ain't got enough cash on me now to get you a good one."

"Thanks, Papa." I didn't want to sound ungrateful, but I'd already missed a chance to ride with the posse. Another two months would be the beginning of winter. Of course, what with Fripp firing me and all, he likely wouldn't be asking me to ride.

But then those wanted posters kept sneaking into my thoughts. Two or three bounties would pay for a house. Emma could live in it and raise her baby there. A bedroom was all I'd ever need.

"How'd you start hunting men, Papa?"

He stopped. "Honey, I ain't talking about stuff like that out here on the street. Another time." Then he opened the tent flap.

Wakum stood at the counter, which was actually a stack of crates with a finished board on top. "Want to do a little shooting today, Blue?"

"Yep. I promised Honey I'd give her a lesson. She told me you could set us up."

Wakum pointed over his shoulder. "Bottles are out back—just set them up in front of the knoll."

Now, a body would think that firing in town might catch the marshal's attention, but we had no such worries, bein's Fripp didn't want to put anyone in jail—especially since he had to feed Pa's prisoner already. Which had gotten me fired. Which had me a mite worried.

Once we'd shot a few cylinders, I asked Pa, "Think I could partner up with you, bein's I don't have a job now?"

Before he could answer, Mayor Tench hollered, "There you are, Honey."

His belly jiggled as he hurried toward us, holding a badge. "I came to give this to you and apologize for the marshal's behavior. You're still deputy of Fry Pan Gulch." He handed the badge to me.

Frankly, I didn't know if I wanted the damned thing.

On the one hand, I liked the weekly pay. But to me, that badge was a symbol of pussyfooting around Fripp all dang day, not arresting owlhoots who needed to be behind bars, and making bad coffee. Actually, I can make good coffee, just not at the marshal's office. But Fripp didn't need to know that. Of course, coffee's about the only thing I knew how to make.

Still and all, there was that seven dollars a week and I didn't have no other job.

"Thanks." I took the badge. Tench stood there eyeballing it in my hand as if he wanted to see me put it on. But I wasn't so sure I would—likely would, but hadn't made up my mind for sure. "We're practicing now. Want I should come by and talk to you later?"

"Um, sure. Might need to give you a raise." He smiled and left.

"Better pin it on," Pa said. "You have a lot to learn before you go hightailing after bounties."

"Like what?"

"See? If you had any idea what the hell was waiting for you out there, you wouldn't have just asked that." He squeezed off five rapid fire shots and five bottles exploded nearly all at once.

Not to be outdone, I set up some more bottles and did the same, but with my right hand. "How do you expect I'll ever find out if you don't tell me?"

"You're as good a shot as me, but that ain't gonna get you any bounties. You need some experience on the trail, and you'll learn a lot by lawdogging, too. Agnes told me about Clem Walton. You done good there."

"Had a dustup at Bougie's Saloon, after Walton."

"Yep, she said that. Each confrontation, you'll learn something new. But just remember, there ain't no town to back you up when you're out in the desert on some owlhoot's trail, and he's just as likely to double back and shoot you as not."

"Ask Blue about the arrest he made in Silver City over in Idaho Territory."

Eh? It was that damned voice again. Now I knew for positive sure it wasn't Papa, and this was the time to give the spooky voice a little test. So I said to Pa, "Tell me about the arrest you made in Silver City."

"Which one?"

"Idaho Territory."

"Ain't no way you could know about that. Who's been tailing me?"

"I just got it in my fool head that you made an entertaining arrest from something Louisa said." Louisa was my older sister, and owned a fancy brothel in Silver City. She hadn't mentioned a thing about Pa in that regard, but it was the only explanation I could think of at the time. "You gonna tell me about it or not?"

"Took some lead in that fracas all on account of I was so green. It was one of my first hunts."

"Who shot you?"

"A feller who called himself Texas Lightning. That's kind of a joke—everyone else called him by his name, Roscoe Peevey. I wasn't even chasing him but he got skeert and took a potshot at me. The only reason he hit me was because I moved in front of the bullet."

"Dammit all, I hit him fair and square," came a voice—the same voice I'd hear now and again—from behind and to the right of me. Now, that caught me up short, but I didn't want to go argufying with some voice in my head in front of Pa. Maybe I was a cartridge shy of a full cylinder.

"So what did you do wrong that got you shot?" I asked.

"Didn't spot all the possible shooters. Don't never disregard no one, even if he's as bad a shot as Roscoe. Anyone there—man, woman, or child—and a few you don't see, just might be laying for you. Since you can't tell, treat every single one of them as if they're aiming for your heart."

We murdered bottles for another thirty minutes and I did my best to stay even with Pa, or even beat him, which was nigh onto impossible.

"You done good, Honey."

Made my day. And week. Hell, maybe all year. What he said was quite a compliment and I had a hard time not busting my buttons with pride, but I kept a cool demeanor.

When we'd murdered the last can, he scooped up the spent casings. "Let's go reload these and clean our shootin' irons."

"I know—never expect you'll have more time later."

"That's right, because more time later just might mean you're gonna have to take aim with a dirty barrel."

"And that ain't safe or accurate."

He ruffled my hair like he done when I was six. "That's my Honey."

Chapter 14

In A Helluva Pickle

After Papa left on the train headed west, I spent most of the next week trying to raise Mama's spirits. As happy as she was to see him, that's how sad she was when he left.

"Mama, you can't hide in your office forever." It pained me to see the frown lines on her face as she sat at her desk, ignoring all the bookkeeping she needed to do. Instead, she chewed on a Dixon pencil and stared out the window.

"It might be two months or even six months before he gets back to Fry Pan Gulch. You can't be moping your life away." I sat in the burgundy velvet chair in front of her desk. "Truth be known, my mood shades to the blue side, too."

"I know, Honey. I'm fixing to work tonight, although Dottie has done a right fine job as hostess. Income is about the same as if I had been tending to business."

"But the men are asking for you. They like having you around."

"I only want to see one man." She shrugged and pushed the letter across the desk. "Your sister wrote me."

"Virginia?" Virginia Thompson was my oldest sister, who generally made a pest of herself all over the West spouting temperance malarkey and bashing up saloons just for the pure-dee hell of it. "She need bail money again?"

"No. Louisa." Mama leaned back in her chair and rested the back of her hand on her forehead. "I'm thinking on visiting. She hasn't been here in a few years and I ain't never seen her place in Silver City."

Louisa had continued in the family profession and was madam at what she said was the finest establishment in Owyhee County. But Idaho Territory was a thousand miles west and even with trains, it took three or four days to get there.

"Sounds like a good idea to me. I miss Louisa, too."

"You want to go with me?"

"Nope, not this time. I have a bunch of things to take care of, including a danged donkey and a pregnant woman."

"Emma isn't your problem. She needs to figure things out on her own—I had to." Mama ended up working in a brothel after some farm boy knocked her up back in Ohio, which was how she got Virginia. "We all have to, one way or another."

Emma might not be my problem but for some reason or other I wanted to help her out. Sassy, though, was definitely my problem, and that blasted mule cluttered up matters.

"I'm still piecing out how to make a living. Once I get that worked out, I'd be happy to take a trip over to Idaho with you—would be fun—but don't ask me to go see Virginia. She ain't nothing but trouble waiting to happen."

Mama chuckled. "The funny thing about that is you're more like Virginia than you are Louisa."

It was good to hear her laugh, even if only a little chuckle. I read my sister's letter. She said everything was fine and she'd be having a baby in August. A baby! Two months from now. I put the letter down on the desk.

"You'll be a grannie!"

"Hard to believe, ain't it. And you'll be Aunt Honey."

"You going to stay with her until she has the baby?"

"Thinking on it. Problem is, I shouldn't be gone that long. Dottie is good, but I don't expect too much of her. It ain't her business." She sighed. "Then again, maybe she'd like to buy the Tasty Chicken and I'll retire."

"In Idaho? But what about Papa? He don't go there very often."

A woman's piercing shriek mixed up with a *hee haw*, and not the donkey kind, had me running to the window to see what was going on in the street. I'd told Sassy and her mule buddy to behave.

"Dang it all. I have to go see what trouble that blasted mule got into now." I jammed my hat on my head and jumped to my feet. "I'll be back and have supper with you," I said as I shut the door and then took off at a dead run for the front door.

Only it wasn't the mule. A lady in her forties dressed in a fancy hat and forest-green dress held a basket hanging over one arm as she wielded a parasol in the other hand. Just when she swung the parasol at Sassy, the mule took a bite out of her bustle. The woman squealed and spun around, bopping the mule on the side of his neck.

"Back away, lady," I said while grabbing her weapon of choice. "Them animals won't hurt you."

"The donkey bit my hat!"

"So she showed poor judgment. Anyone can tell them flowers ain't real."

"And the mule—"

"You have on a green dress. Must have looked mighty tasty to him." I turned to Sassy and pointed down the road. "Git on home, you two. Now." They plodded down the street, heads hanging and ears drooping.

She pursed her lips and glared at my badge. "Deputy marshal? You must be Honey Beaulieu."

I nodded but didn't roll my eyes. How many folks in these parts was ignorant enough to pin on a badge? "Yes, ma'am. And you?"

"Mrs. Shangle. My husband is the carpenter."

I knew him—had played poker with him many times. Surly old cuss. I couldn't tell her I was sorry, for she was likely sorry enough already. "Met him a time or two. You must have nice furniture in your house."

"Not really." She sighed. "He sells all the nicest pieces." Then she straightened her shoulders. "Who owns these animals? He owes me a new dress and hat."

"I do. Well, the donkey, anyhow. Don't you worry yourself none, ma'am—I'll pay to get your dress fixed and even buy you a new garden for you to tote around on top of your head."

There went my rifle, dammit all.

"Honey!" Emma hurried toward me, holding her skirts with one hand and waving. That was all I needed—first a lady with a mule bite out of her bustle and now a weepy pregnant woman. Her cheeks glowed pink and she had a wide smile, which sorta made me suspicious on account of she hadn't done nothing but cry since the day I met her in the storeroom.

Then I got an idea. "You good with a needle?"

"Better than most, but not as good as Madame Francois at the dressmaker's shop."

Madame Francois was about as French as Sassy was, and everyone knew it, but they didn't say anything to her. She likely thought she could charge more using a French name.

"Think you could fix a rip in this lady's bustle?"

"Why certainly. A little reweaving, an extra pucker here and there, and no one would ever know."

"Fetch Mama's sewing bag, then. We'll go to my room at the livery."

"I have my own." Emma took off as fast as her skirts would allow.

"The livery?" Mrs. Shangle's eyebrows raised nearly to her hairline. "I can't go to the livery. There's..." She whisked her parasol in a circle as if leading the local brass band. "...animals in there."

"Including Sassy and the mule, but my room is in the loft. Don't worry, we can heft you and your bustle up the ladder."

"I would never!"

"Or we could go to the Tasty Chicken. Your choice."

"The livery's fine. I'll need something to cover up my backside. It's embarrassing enough standing on the boardwalk with my petticoats showing."

"They don't show at all. He didn't bite all the way through the cloth—just ripped the ruffle. It don't look fancy, but your south side is covered as good as your north."

"And my hat?"

"We'll pass by the milliner's shop on the way." Which

dang neart killed me, paying for a silly hat that didn't even shade her face good, what with all the other stuff I needed to buy. Like a rifle.

Ten minutes later, I shoved two hard earned bucks across the millinery counter.

I turned to the woman who'd been the object of the mule's munching. "You square with Emma fixin' you up?"

Mrs. Shangle lifted her chin—all of them, actually. "I'm a fair woman. You'll hear no more from me if she does a good job." She adjusted the tilt of her bonnet and tied the chin straps in a bow near her left ear. Lopsided anything made me plumb streaky but I didn't say nothing.

"Let's go get you fixed up." I headed toward the livery and expected her to follow, which she and Emma did, sewing bag in hand. The girl skipped to catch up with me. I likely only had a couple years on her but she seemed dreadful young to already be having a baby.

"I enjoy sewing. I hope Mrs. Shangle likes my work."

"You do your best and maybe you can set yourself up in business. Madame Francois turns customers away on account of her being so busy."

"I know, but she enjoys doing that. I doubt she'd much cotton to someone horning in on her territory."

"It's a free country." Damned expensive country, though. My pockets was getting lighter by the minute.

And I still didn't have a horse or a rifle.

* * *

Mrs. Shangle left the livery happy as a cat with a fresh-killed mouse, and Emma said she was gonna look for a job. She could work for a few months before she started to show, and a little money would help matters a lot.

I went to the office, where everything was exactly the same as when I left it. The marshal hadn't even bothered to come by for a cup of coffee, near as I could tell.

Fripp had spent the entire week getting over his mad at me by frequenting the Tasty Chicken. Besides his irritation with me, he was still pissed off about Roxbury stealing his horse. Said it would take him a month of Sundays to save enough money to buy another one. I kept my counsel about the high cost of his whoring habits, even with all the free pokes he got.

Come suppertime, my stomach grumbled. I locked up the marshal's office and headed for some good food at the Tasty Chicken, where unfortunately I'd likely find Fripp. Sassy and the mule dogged my every step, which was bothersome because they slobbered on my neck, but a whole lot better than them running around finding trouble.

That blasted mule was a big critter. I could pass Sassy off as a pet, but the mule caused a little excitement now and again, and the incident with Mrs. Shangle was only the start. If I didn't know better, I'd say he was trying to keep my attention, but dang, it would put me in a more agreeable disposition if he'd quit nipping ladies' bustles. Some of them ladies wasn't all bustle—those gals got especially het up. He needed to stop that old business.

I'd been doing a lot of thinking about that critter.

"Ain't no tamer mule to be found," a man said.

"I don't see no reason why I couldn't ride him." Then I turned around and tried to find the man what was talking to me—that same voice that had me spooked. Not a soul was anywhere near.

"If he didn't have such a bad reputation for bucking

good riders off," the old man's voice said, "he'd go for a right high price—a big black racing mule, fast as the wind and sturdy as a petrified tree stump."

I didn't dare say a thing back. Folks would think I was plumb loco for yammering on at nothing but thin air. Still, that voice made sense, so I set course back to the livery. Supper could wait.

Chapter 15

Gonna Ride That Mule

Supper waited, all right, but not for me to ride the mule.

"Honey!" Emma flagged me down as I was on my way to the livery. "I got a job!"

"Where at?"

"Golden Ruhl Mercantile. Mrs. Ruhl hired me to make alterations on ready-made dresses and such." The whole danged town had heard she was in a family way, and who done it, too, but most folks pretended they didn't know it. "And she also offered to rent me the room above the store."

"That's fine news. I expect you'll want to be moving there soon."

"This evening, if you'll help."

She didn't have much but we got her situated. Seeing her so happy made putting off my plans worth it.

* * *

The next morning, I woke up amidst all of Wheat's plunking on horseshoes—he made a hell of a racket, which was good because I never slept in and hadn't been late for work once. Today, though, I just might be late on account of I decided to ride that damned mule whether he wanted rode or not. Wheat had said no one could ride him, but I remembered Pa saying that there was nary a horse alive that couldn't be rode. The mule wasn't a horse but I put him in the same category.

While Wheat was occupied, I fed both Sassy and the mule. They munched away not paying me no mind, so I fetched a saddle from the tack room. Wheat shouldn't disapprove on account of if I got the mule ready to ride, he'd go for a good price. Of course I was hoping I could buy the mule for cheap, bein's I'd spent too danged much money on ladies' hats and bustles after he'd made such a pest of himself.

It occurred to me that I should give the mule a name, but since he wasn't mine, it seemed pointless, so I didn't. I grabbed a sturdy-looking saddle and lugged it down to the mule's stall.

Wheat stopped his hammering. "What you doing with that saddle?"

"Gonna ride that mule."

"You ain't gonna ride him far. And anyway, that ain't a mule saddle."

"You got tack for him?"

"Yep, but you don't need it, bein's you said you don't ride."

"I'm going to ride him, or at least try."

"Tack room—back left corner. It's the fancy one."

"I see that big sorrel's back."

"Yep, the U.S. deputy marshal is on the hunt for Roxbury. The bounty's up to two hundred and fifty dollars." He untied his blacksmith apron and put on his hat.

Sam Lancaster. I remembered Wheat talking about the U.S. deputy marshal before, although I'd yet to meet the man.

"Where you goin'?" I asked Wheat.

"I'm calling Doc just in case."

"Ain't gonna need him." Sassy and me headed for the tack room. I'd never been in there before, nor had I been around animals all that much before I moved to the livery, other than the two-legged kind, and they were hard to bridle. Not that you'd want to—I'd rather just leave them run wild.

The tack room had every sort of strap imaginable hanging from a line of half-driven nails in the walls, and several saddles rested astride a row of sawhorses. Shelves on the side wall held harness parts and pieces. The place was orderly but had so much stuff in it that it still boggled my mind some.

I wound my way past the saddles and dodged the harnesses to the back left corner of the room. A skinny saddle rested on a barrel, and a bunch of other straps beside it, with a bridle laid on top. I reckoned this must be the tack for the racing mule so I hauled it out to the main area of the barn where Sassy and the mule waited for me.

Just so Sassy didn't think I was ignoring her, I put her pack saddle on her and loaded her with a bag of oats and a couple full canteens—enough for her to know she was carrying something, but no more. Then I bridled the mule. He didn't give me no trouble whatsoever. Encouraged by his gentleness and calmness, I put the saddle blanket on and patted him a bit, then I hefted the saddle onto his back. He didn't even flinch.

There was some straps and whatnot that I had no idea what to do with so I tightened the cinch and left all the other stuff in a neat pile beside what was supposed to be his stall. The one that he was not ever in.

So the U.S. deputy marshal was after Roxbury, eh? The bounty had gone up on Roxbury since Fripp had reported him as a horse thief. I could use that two hundred and fifty dollars. I reckoned the hunt would take ten dollars' worth of supplies and I would have better than two hundred dollars left over.

That was enough to buy me a rifle and get Emma situated in a house for when the baby came. If the mule worked out, I could buy him and then I wouldn't need a horse. Or maybe Wheat would rent him to me.

I led the mule out of the livery and Sassy followed. Neither one of them seemed a bit nervous about the whole situation, but my belly buzzed. I reckoned if I could get on the mule, though, all I had to do from there was hang on until he tuckered himself out.

Wheat had come back, and when I turned around to look, he leaned against the livery doorframe with his arms crossed, watching me. I have to say, that made me nervous, but I wasn't about to let him know it.

"All right, mule, let's go for a ride."

I situated the reins over the mule's neck, then put my left foot in the stirrup. He didn't do a thing and didn't seem concerned, so I put a little of my weight in the stirrup like I'd seen cowhands do on green broke horses. That didn't bother him none either, so I went ahead and slung my right leg over the top and sat in the saddle, holding the reins in one hand and the saddle horn in the other. I know it ain't manly to hang onto the saddle horn, but I ain't a man.

We weren't going anywhere fast, so I nudged his sides with the heels of my boots. Next thing I knew, I was flat on my back on the ground, looking up at his chin and neck, with the saddle still between my legs.

It happened so fast I didn't have time to think. But I got up and dusted myself off, glared at the mule, and caught the one rein that was dangling.

"We're gonna have a set-to, and when we're all done with that nonsense, you're gonna let me ride you."

Soon as I managed to get some air in my lungs, I saddled the mule again.

"You might use the britchin," Wheat said. "Keeps the saddle from sliding forward."

"I don't know what a britchin is."

"It's them straps what you left off. Go fetch 'em and I'll help you."

After I brought back the pile of leather straps, Wheat set to fastening them to the sides of the saddle.

"This here piece," he held up a wider strap, "goes around his butt, under his tail. Otherwise, any little jump or sudden stop, and the saddle would fly right over his head, as you just found out. This holds it in place."

When Wheat was done, he handed me the reins. "You sure you want to ride him?"

"He follows me everywhere I go—him and Sassy. Might as well try to ride him. He's tame enough. Might want to buy him."

"Honey, I'd try to talk some sense into your head if it'd do a damn bit of good."

"Well, it won't." I led the mule to the middle of the road. "I'm riding this mule. Can't be too hard."

* * *

Riding might not be too hard but the ground sure as

hell was. The sky sure was pretty—bright blue with fluffy white clouds. Of course, I wasn't too keen on seeing the sky for the second time. Not from flat on my back.

He'd gone about three strides when I felt his muscles bunch up and then off I went again. With a little luck, no one had seen except for Wheat. Once I got some air, I stood and dusted myself off.

"Ready for another go?" At least the mule hadn't run off. Instead, he'd just stood there and waited while I collected myself.

The next try, we managed to get a ways down the street before he deposited me in the dirt. That time, I came down hard on one knee, and damn, that hurt. But I got right back on. We'd get a few more steps before he'd take to hopping and buck me off again.

I tried to get him turned around and headed back to the stable, but he took off for downtown. Right in front of the Golden Ruhl, the mule skidded to a stop on all fours, and I landed upside down in a pickle barrel. Banged my head, bit my tongue, and dang neart drowned in vinegar. Now that pissed me off. Next thing I knew, someone lifted me out of the barrel and stood me up.

Eye-height to his badge, I'd finally come face to face with the U.S. deputy marshal, without a doubt the handsomest man I ever did see. Leastways, his chest was. Then again, it could've been the pickle juice in my eyes.

Dark hair, strong jaw, damned nice shoulders, and he raised one eyebrow when he grinned. He had all his teeth and they was clean, too. His long muscled legs, bowed just a bit from days in the saddle. I could see why he needed such a big horse. Sam Lancaster would be a welcome customer at the Tasty Chicken. Then again, for some stupid reason I didn't want him to go there.

He handed me my hat. "I think this is yours."

"Um, yeah." Damn, never in all my twenty-two years had a man tripped up my tongue like this one. Good thing he was riding out.

"I see you're the law in this town." His voice sounded low and smooth. I could listen to him talk all night.

Remembering Fripp's tone when he talked to the reporter at Bougie's Saloon, I said, "Ain't much of a law in Fry Pan Gulch, but I do my best." I jammed the hat on my head right over the pickle juice dripping from my braid, and ears, and chin. What a sight I was, and embarrassed as all git-out.

He offered a handshake. "Sam Lancaster, U.S. deputy marshal."

I swiped the bread and butter pickle juice from my palm onto the leg of my britches and blinked the stinging vinegar from my eyes, then shook his hand. "Honey Beaulieu, Fry Pan Gulch deputy marshal." The mule brayed. "Best I be going now."

Out of sheer desperation, I grabbed a few pickles from my shirt and offered them to the mule. He gobbled them up like candy.

Lancaster chuckled. "Never saw a mule that'd eat pickles."

Thad Ruhl came bustling out of the store. "You ruined a whole barrel of pickles, Honey. I'll be expecting payment for that."

"You'll be getting it. Keep your shirt on." I plucked out the pickles from the top of my shirt, then mounted the mule. "Best you order another barrel right away."

Then I rode off—left the handsome Lancaster standing in front of the Golden Ruhl, on account of I had no idea what else to do or even where to go. I did know that I had to get my sorry butt out of there and away from the U.S. deputy marshal, who stood akimbo laughing at me. I felt like a real ass.

Which reminded me of Sassy. I whistled and she came a'running.

"I don't expect you like pickles, too."

Then I patted the mule on his neck. "How come you haven't bucked me off yet?"

The mule farted. That did it, I named him Pickles.

Chapter 16

Except For The Honey Buns

Clem's drinking finally got the best of him as well as an unlucky fellow at the Tasty Chicken poker table. And for once, Marshal Fripp wasn't there.

Fripp and me was shootin' the breeze in the office when Nolan Radison busted in the door.

"Come quick—there's been a shooting at the Tasty Chicken!"

The marshal stood quicker than usual and grabbed a rifle off the rack. "Who?"

"Don't know the fellow. Clem shot him when he accused him of cheating."

"Who accused who?" Fripp chambered some rounds.

"The stranger accused Clem. I wasn't there, but I was told Clem jumped up from his chair and shot the man in the chest. They took the feller to Doc's but he likely don't have many breaths left."

"Where's Clem?"

"He lit out before the poor man even hit the floor, according to Agnes."

I could only imagine what she was feeling. Mama don't take to shooting and the like. At the first sign of trouble, the customer was thrown in the street. She didn't hire no bouncers because she didn't need to. At the crook of her finger, five gentlemen—well, they wasn't all that gentle—would take care of the situation. But a shooting? That would upset her. Through the years there'd been all manner of ruckus at the whorehouse, but never a killing, and the way Nolan talked, that's what we had.

Fripp put on his hat. "Honey, rustle up a posse. You'll have to rent a horse for me, and take my rounds later."

His orders was getting a mite tiresome. For one thing, he never went on his rounds—I did. For another, I wasn't about to miss a second posse as Fry Pan Gulch deputy. And third, I wanted Clem Walton's hide. "How about I ride with the posse?"

"You ain't got a horse, either, plus you don't know the first thing about trailing a criminal. Best you stay here and let me take care of man's business."

That rumpled my feathers, to say the least. I'd been taking care of stupid men's business for a couple months. "I can ride the mule."

"Until he decides to dump your ass in a barrel of pickles. Now get out of here. I want Wakum, Wheat, and anyone else who might want to go."

Nolan stood with his hand on the doorknob. "I'll go."

"Wheat'll likely want you to tend the livery. Don't know as if you can hit the broad side of a barn if you was standing on it, though."

"You're right. I'll tend the livery." Nolan left muttering to himself. Fripp had no call to say what he said since he had no idea if Radison was a decent shot or not. I reckoned he'd be a good man to have on our side, though. More useful than Fripp.

As it turned out, Wakum wouldn't go, nor Wheat, either. As Wheat said, "I got better things to do with my day than chasin' after some addlebrained shanny who can't keep his pecker in his britches or his iron in his holster."

No amount of wheedling would change Wheat's mind.

"Best he stay gone, as far as I'm concerned." Then he stoked up the bellows, so that was the end of the conversation.

If Fripp wanted Wheat bad enough, he could come to the livery and ask like he should've done in the first dang place. I felt the same as Wheat—good riddance to Clem Walton and may he never come back. He hadn't done one blasted thing right in the ten years the Waltons had been living near Fry Pan Gulch, and him knocking up a respectable gal like Emma really fried my bacon.

When I got back, Fripp tossed a paper on my desk. "Got a wire from Sam Lancaster, U.S. deputy marshal. He'll be riding with me, so make damned sure Wheat gives me a good-looking horse."

Sam Lancaster was the man who hauled me out of the pickle barrel. I could tell right off he wasn't a big bag of air like Fripp. He had that lazy kind of manner that didn't fool a soul—deadly—just like my pa. And damn if he wasn't as handsome, if more so. As tall or taller, too.

Eight days had passed since I'd seen him for that brief but embarrassing time, and yet he horned his way into my thoughts more often than I'd 'fess up to.

"Archie Ruhl wanted to go but his ma won't let him. Wheat ain't going and neither is Wakum, so I'll go." I sat back in my chair. "The mule's all saddled and so's your rental horse."

"You're staying here. Got to leave someone in charge."

Now that was a new one. Before Mayor Tench made me deputy marshal, Fripp had left Wakum in charge when he left town. Which wasn't often, on account of the Tasty Chicken was in town, and Fripp never strayed far from it.

"Might you stay and I'll go. I expect you'd rather sleep on a nice soft bed than on the dirt."

"You're right about the bed, but you ain't going so get that out of your head." He handed me a list. "Head over to the Golden Ruhl and have Thad get this stuff together. I'll pick it up once I get my horse." As I was about to get up, he said, "I'm taking your donkey for packing."

I sat back again. "No you ain't."

"The hell I ain't."

"Rent your own pack animal. Sassy goes where I go, and you said I'm staying here."

He pounded his fist on his desk, which I hoped hurt his knuckles. "Damn it all, Honey, are you the deputy or not?"

"According to Mayor Tench, I am."

He huffed at that remark, bein's he never wanted me for deputy in the first place. "Then I'm taking the donkey."

"I'll arrest you for stealing if you do."

"Then I'm taking the rental out of your pay."

"We'll see what Tench has to say about that."

Behind Fripp stood Sam Lancaster, feet apart, arms folded across his chest, and a silly grin on his face. I hadn't noticed him come in—he'd likely heard every word we'd said. As Fripp whirled around to head to the livery, he ran right square into Lancaster, who didn't budge even a smidgeon.

"Ready to go?" the U.S. deputy asked.

"Not quite. Ran into a snag."

He sure had—one well over six feet tall. But I didn't laugh.

Lancaster winked at me. "I see." He went to the stove and poured himself a cup of coffee. "While you're doing your errands, I'll stay here and have Deputy Beaulieu brief me about the shooting."

"I can do that while we're in the saddle."

"That, too." Lancaster put his cup on Fripp's desk and sat. "For now, I want her version."

"She has to pick up my supplies."

Lancaster took a slow slurp of coffee, leaned back, and put his boots on the town marshal's desk. "I was always of the opinion that a man ought to buy his own supplies—make sure everything's good quality and all there."

You can't not like a man who'd best Fripp in such a manner.

"Careful with him, Honey. He's a smooth talker."

Damn, that voice again! Maybe I had gone barmy. I better watch it—the town drunk heard voices. That could be me.

After Fripp left, Lancaster asked, "You and that mule getting along any better?"

I loved the sound of his voice. "We have an understanding. I do what he wants, and we get along just fine. He lets me ride him now."

"Sounds like your training is coming along just fine, then. Not so sure about the mule, but he sounds like a good teacher."

"His name's Pickles. If I feed him a bread and butter pickle before I mount up, he won't buck me off."

"I expect that's all right in town, but if you're riding

with a posse, there's a big shortage of bread and butter pickles out in the wide open spaces."

"He likes honey buns, too, and anyway, Fripp don't seem to be in no hurry for me to ride with his posse."

"I have to say, I like honey buns myself." When he grinned I threw the pot of posies at him.

He caught the pot but the posies flew everywhere. One landed on his ear.

Just so he didn't get no wrong ideas, I said, "You get your honey buns down the street at Tex's Café."

Just then, Mama walked in looking a bit frazzled, especially with the gray showing through her hennaed hair. "Fripp gone to catch that four-flusher yet?"

"Not yet, Mama. He's fixin' to go, though—buying supplies now, I expect."

"You riding with them?"

"Nope." I pointed at Lancaster, who'd stood when she'd walked in. The flower had fallen from his ear to his shoulder. "He is."

Mama looked him up and down, then glanced at me, then back at him for another once-over. I hadn't seen that expression on her face since I was ten years old and she'd chastised me for eating an entire cherry pie.

"And you are?"

I stepped between them. "This is Sam Lancaster, U.S. deputy marshal." I turned to him and held Mama's arm. "This is Agnes Thompson, proprietor of the Tasty Chicken."

Mama offered her hand and he kissed the back of it. "Howdy, ma'am."

"Nice to meet you. I don't remember you coming to

my establishment."

"No, ma'am, I haven't had the pleasure."

"We offer women, poker, faro, and the finest food in Fry Pan Gulch."

"Except for the honey buns?"

Mama pointed her gloved finger and waggled it at him. "You stay away from my Honey's buns, big boy. You can have the ones at Tex's Café."

"So your daughter told me."

Sassy took that moment to stick her head through the open window and bray, bless her heart.

"I have to feed my donkey." I lit out of there as if my hair was on fire. In fact, it just might've been, the way my face burned. Maybe not riding with the posse was all for the best. I would've hated to put up with that man all hours of the day and night. Or maybe...

Well, damn. My thoughts was leading me down the garden path.

Sassy nuzzled me and I patted her on the neck. "What we need is to get out of this town." But even though the train came and left every day, with people getting on and off—mostly on—I didn't have no idea where they went to or what they did once they got there. Fry Pan Gulch was my whole world, so I dismissed the notion as fast as it had come.

Emma came out of the Golden Ruhl, carrying several packages, with Archie Ruhl following, loaded with even more bundles.

"I heard about the shooting. Are you riding with the posse?" she asked.

"Fripp wants me to stay here." That still left a bad

taste in my mouth. "The U.S. deputy marshal's going, though. They'll catch Clem."

"They surely will." Emma nudged Archie. "We best get Mrs. Tench's order to her."

The two of them hurried down the street. Emma didn't seem too tore up over Clem Walton, what with him hightailing out on her and all. Archie, the Ruhls' twenty-year-old son, likely had something to do with that. He seemed plumb mashed up over Emma even though he knew she had Clem's bun in the oven. I could see why—Emma was a pretty little thing and had a sunny disposition when she wasn't moping about the fix she'd got herself in.

Archie was a strapping fellow, taller than his pa, and a gentle soul. I'd have laid odds that he'd be a good father to Emma's baby if he took a notion. How his folks would take to the matter, I had no idea.

What I did know was that he wanted to be on the posse that Marshal Fripp called, and Archie's mama wasn't too keen on the notion.

"But you could catch Ed Roxbury. That'd put over two hundred dollars in your purse after expenses."

Most folks' thoughts sound like themselves. Why this old man's voice kept getting in my head was anyone's guess. But blast it all anyway, he had a point. Roxbury was still on the loose. Money on the hoof. I could buy the mule, the saddle, the rifle, and have money left over to get Emma settled in her own place if I caught Roxbury.

Not a bad idea at all.

Chapter 17

Don't Kick Up Dust

"No, Honey." Wheat hefted a sack of grain on his left shoulder with no more effort than a normal man would lift his hat. "I ain't selling a mule to you that I can't trust, and I don't trust this critter no matter what you named him."

The critter in question nibbled on my braid. I pushed him away for the dozenth time, for all the good it did.

"Oh, c'mon, Wheat. I've worked with Pickles for the last couple of weeks and can ride him just fine."

"When you ain't flat on your back looking at his belly."

"I admit, ain't nary a part of me that's not sore and bruised, but I figured that mule out. Give him a pickle—has to be a bread and butter pickle—and I can ride him." Didn't give him a pickle... well, I'd eat dirt every time, but Wheat didn't need to hear that.

"What if you ain't got a bread and butter pickle?"

"Last week, I offered him a honey bun and he liked that. Seems as though he'll do dang neart anything for a sweet." Otherwise, he wouldn't do nothing at all but buck and be contrary. Ornery critter.

Of course, it looked like Sam Lancaster would do about anything for a honey bun, too, but I didn't even want to think about him. I had other problems—such as getting me a ride. And I wanted the racing mule.

Stubborn as he was, Pickles had wormed his way into my heart and I'd rode him every day, with Sassy trotting happily alongside. Pickles could run like the wind, though, and when he did, my poor little donkey had a hell of a time keeping up. But me and Pickles would stop every now and again, and Sassy would eventually catch us. I'd let her rest and then we'd move on.

Now, I just needed Wheat to sell the mule to me and give me a bill of sale.

"Aw, Wheat. He hasn't throwed me for a day and a half. I think he's broke good now."

"Looks to me like you're the one what's broke."

"There is that. But Pickles is a fine mule and I do trust him." I dragged my toe through the dust on the livery floor. "Sorta. I know he won't leave me high and dry. He won't run off like most horses and mules will."

Wheat took the grain down to the other end of the livery, then came back to the tack room and started fiddling with a heap of harness parts. I followed him, thinking he was ignoring me, but finally he said, "Fifty dollars, then. Cash on the barrelhead."

"I ain't got fifty dollars." Or a barrelhead. "How about thirty?"

He shook his head so I took another angle at it.

"Might you could rent him to me?"

"Nope. Your mama would whoop me."

"She don't whoop hard—not unless you've paid for it." Which was supposed to be a joke, since Mama didn't take customers, but Wheat didn't crack a smile.

"I'll think on it. Now let me get to my work here."

"Rent him to me for two weeks and I'll pay you in full,

and for the tack, too."

"That's what I'm selling, the tack. I'm giving you the damned mule—I'll have the bill of sale ready by morning. Now get on with you."

* * *

When I got back to the office with my good news, Wakum sat at the marshal's desk smoking a cigar as he cleaned a rifle.

"What's the pleasure of your visit?" I asked.

"Fripp left me in charge."

I could feel the red fog of mad rise through me fast as one of them dust devils. I was the deputy marshal—Fripp knew he should put me in charge. "Did he say why?"

"He's still sore at you, I expect." Wakum stood and gathered his gun cleaning supplies. "I also have work to do, so I'm putting you in charge."

"Don't bother. I quit." I tossed my badge on Fripp's desk. "Gonna catch me a Roxbury. I reckon it'll take me a week, and two hundred dollars is a lot better pay for a week's work than seven."

"In that case, you'll need this rifle I just cleaned for you. Pay me for it at the end of the month. Best you stop by the shop and pick up a couple boxes of cartridges—practice with one box and take the other with you."

"You ain't surprised that I'm going?"

"Honey, I do believe the only surprised person around this joint is you. Wheat, Ruhl, and I have a pool."

A pool? They'd been betting on when I'd leave? "Well, damn." I picked up the rifle and looked down the sights. The piece was balanced just right for me. "Who won?"

"Me. Wheat reckoned you'd leave last week, once you got that mule rode. Ruhl's out—he said you'd wait until Fripp got back."

"If Wheat would've sold Pickles to me last week, he might've won."

"Nope, on account of you wouldn't be going even now if Fripp hadn't done you dirty by appointing me interim marshal."

"There is that."

"You be careful on the trail. Watch your back. Don't kick up dust, and don't ever go nowhere without at least two full canteens of water."

"Hell, I don't even know how to track a man."

"You'll learn. With Roxbury, you'll have to head the same direction he left, then ask folks if they've seen him. They'll turn him over to you, as obnoxious as he's been."

"Papa says he follows tracks."

"Sometimes, but Roxbury left on the train headed east from what I heard. Ain't a way in the world to track him lest he throws some sort of sign out the window—torn jacket or the like. Might even have got off the train and headed cross-country." He picked a cleaning rod out of his bag of tools and gave it to me. "Keep your rifle clean, the sun off your face, and stay dry at night. I reckon you ought to run a full pack on Sassy, what with you bein' green and all."

Wakum poured himself some coffee. "Want some?"

"Eh, not now. I expect I ought to get my supplies together and get out of Fry Pan Gulch before Fripp decides to come back. Right about now I'd like to smooth out his wrinkled face with Wheat's anvil."

* * *

Along about two miles out of town, my belly started to churn, mostly on account of I hadn't had time to think about what was in store for me until now. Sassy carried all manner of supplies Thad Ruhl had decided I'd need. He should know since he'd outfitted many a lawman, as well as bounty hunters, including Pa, miners, and mountain men.

Wakum damn neart talked my ear off what with all the advice he had, and Wheat gave me a pair of chaps, then hovered over me like an old woman. Mama said she'd see me for supper once I came to my right mind later in the day. Well, I had. I wanted that two hundred and fifty dollars.

Thad sold me the whole raft of supplies on credit including two ropes just in case I actually caught someone. Debt made me nearly as nervous as being out of Fry Pan Gulch, but I was bound and determined to pay him back long before the four weeks when the bill came due.

Pickles hadn't given me no trouble—could've been because Thad loaded a gallon of bread and butter pickles onto Sassy's pack. Once I repacked in the morning, I'd put them in Pickles' saddlebag. Seemed to me like he ought to carry them, considering he insisted on eating them in order to carry me. I'm tall but I don't weigh much. Pound for pound, Sassy carried more than Pickles did.

Neither the donkey nor the mule much cared, as far as I could see. They trotted right along as if we three was born to go on adventures together. They might be right. Fry Pan Gulch didn't offer much, and it was time to see new territory, scary as the unknown was.

We headed east, on account of Thad had heard

Roxbury had boarded the train to Cheyenne. I didn't know a soul in Cheyenne other than Sam Lancaster, and he wasn't there. Whether that made me glad or sad varied by the minute. The hairs on the back of my neck said to stay away from him, but something else a whole lot stronger pulled me to him.

But I needed to keep my mind on Roxbury—a wily fox who'd slipped away from some damned good lawmen. Why I thought I could catch him when they couldn't hadn't occurred to me until now. Mama was likely right and I'd be back at the Tasty Chicken before nightfall.

* * *

The endless rolling hills and the vastness of the country made me feel mighty small. As far as I could look, there was more of the same—rolling hills with grass and brush, and mountains in the background. I wondered what those mountains would be like up close, and I aimed to find out some day.

The afternoon was hotter than usual and glaringly bright so I was grateful for my big floppy hat and the extra canteens, which I filled at every opportunity as Wakum had told me to do. I stayed near the train tracks, and not for the first time wondered if it would've been smarter to stay another day in Fry Pan Gulch and catch the train myself. Where I'd have found the money for a ticket is another matter. As the saying went, grass was growin' under my feet, and it was time to leave. So I left.

A couple hours later, I pulled Pickles to a stop near a nice little stream with some tall grass along the bank for the animals to graze. I was happy to get off the mule, for I wasn't used to long hours in the saddle, and my sit-down was going numb.

I unbuckled, untied, and unfastened Sassy's pack, taking care to remember how to put it all back together again—not just what was packed and where, but where all those infernal straps went. Pickles held still while I unsaddled him, then did me the favor of shaking sweat all over me.

Wheat and Wakum had both insisted that I hobble the donkey and mule, but I couldn't get rid of them if I wanted to so I didn't see what use there was. And likely, it would just make the both of them mad at me.

A few minutes after I got the fire started and the coffee on, a rider approached on a ragged bay that looked run half to death, then stopped about fifty feet away.

"Hello, the camp!" he hollered.

My shooting hand was at the ready. Country manners didn't allow me to turn him away, but I wished he hadn't come.

"Set and light," I hollered back.

He ground-tied his horse and walked to the campfire. First thing he did was waggle his eyebrows at me. "I sure didn't know I'd find a pretty lady out here."

His friendly greeting didn't feel so friendly to me, and I ignored his remark, but much more of his nonsense and he'd get a fast case of lead poisoning. "Coffee won't be ready for another five minutes yet."

"What's a girl like you doing out here in the wild country?"

"Minding my own business."

"Seen anyone?"

"You."

"I'm looking for a man named Ed Roxbury. Seen him?"

"Back in Fry Pan Gulch. He left town a few weeks ago."

"If I find that son of a bitch, I'm gonna string him up."

"Get in line."

"You after him?"

The stranger didn't need to know my business. "The marshal wants him." I hadn't lied. Fripp wanted Roxbury so bad, he'd probably even trade him for one or two free pokes at the Tasty Chicken, and that's goin' some. But the marshal, and the U.S. marshal, too, were after Clem Walton at the moment.

"What charges?"

"I don't rightly know, but horse thieving is at the top of the list. What's your cause for chasing him?"

"He swindled a buddy of mine."

The stranger had finally said something I believed. Not that I was of a mind to help him any. "Sorry about that."

"Nice mule you got there."

"We get along."

"Looks like a thoroughbred mare threw him."

"Don't have no idea, but he's fast, all right."

"I wouldn't mind having a mule like that." He stood. "Best I be on my way. Got to find a camping spot before nightfall."

Good riddance. But my hackles was still up, and I didn't exactly trust that he'd be leaving.

Chapter 18

I Don't Share Bacon

The stranger only pretended to leave, just as I'd reckoned. By the time I'd fried some bacon and heated up the beans, Pickles and Sassy both commenced to braying and stomping something fierce. Branches crackled and then I heard a thump.

A man groaned. I didn't want my bacon to burn so took it off the fire and covered it before I went to see what all the commotion was about. Knowing Sassy and Pickles, they didn't need any help to take care of unwelcome visitors that might happen to come around, so I wasn't in much of a hurry.

By the time I got to where they was snorting and stomping, they'd pretty well taken care of the situation. Sassy stood guard over the poor owlhoot, and kicked him every time he moved. Pickles, saddled and bridled, which he wasn't not over twenty minutes ago, chased off the man's horse, although it looked to me as if the horse was all too happy to go. I'd have to find him later and unsaddle him so he had a fair chance to join up with a wild horse herd.

I held my Peacemaker on the sneaky visitor with my left hand and patted Sassy on the withers with the other. Looked all the world like he was trying to make off with my mule, but Pickles had other ideas on the matter.

"Throw your weapons off toward that bush over there." I cocked my head toward the bush I meant so he had no misunderstanding. "That includes your hideout gun."

"My arm's broke."

"You got two of 'em. Get busy."

After I coaxed him a little by cocking my six-shooter, he finally got the job done, although I had to remind him about his hideout gun.

"Sit up and take off your boots."

"Only got one arm."

"Figure it out."

He took a little too long so I shot the toe of his boot off.

"Damn, woman!"

"I'll shoot your own toe off next shot. Get busy."

He seemed to be able to use his broken arm just fine. Of course, a knife fell out of his boot, which didn't surprise me none. I kicked it away before he got any foolish notions.

"You sit here real quiet-like while I fetch the rope." To Sassy, I said, "You keep him right there. I'll be right back."

"I ought to shoot that ass," the scoundrel muttered.

"I ought to shoot your ass. Now, shut up."

The second I turned my back, he must've done something Sassy didn't like on account of she let him have it with both hind hooves. That put him out. I got the rope and tied him up real tight—hands and feet. But what in the world was I gonna do with him? A prisoner would only slow me down.

First thing I did was check the wad of wanted posters that Wakum had stuffed in my saddlebag. The stranger didn't resemble any of them. Too bad, for it would've been a whole lot easier to take him in for bounty than to chase over half the country for Roxbury.

By the time I fetched the rope, Pickles trotted back, and the fellow's horse was nowhere in sight.

The stranger sat up, rubbing his head and whimpering. When he saw me, he hollered, "That damned mule run my horse off!"

"Good for him. I ain't got no use for fellers who treat horses the way you do."

"What're you planning for me? I ain't got charges against me."

"I'd charge you with mule thievin' if I was of a mind to, but I don't have time for that. Best you shut your pie hole or I'll stuff your stinkin' sock in it."

The last rays of sun would be gone in another thirty minutes, and with a half moon rising, there wouldn't be much light for long. I didn't want this man on the loose while I was trying to sleep, but having him in my camp didn't exactly set so good, either. He'd do less harm if I kept him until morning, though, even if that meant I had to share my beans. He wasn't getting no bacon, though. I don't share bacon.

I ate all the bacon, half the beans, and washed it down with a cup of hot coffee.

"You gonna let me starve to death?" He hocked up a loogy and spat.

"You can have some beans. Open up and I'll shovel 'em in."

"I druther feed myself."

"I druther you not be here at all. You want some of my beans, or not?"

"Damn, you're a tough woman."

"That ain't tough—that's smart."

He opened his mouth. I hated for him to get his slobbers on my spoon, but I'd wash it real good later, so I fed him. Not as much as he wanted, but I damned well wasn't about to waste an extra can of beans on an unwelcome visitor. Besides, I had less than ten dollars in coins and I had to spend my money frugally. For now.

That two hundred and some dollars had been spent a dozen ways already. Looked to me like I'd have to haul in a lot of bounties just to get myself set up.

When I laid out my bedroll by the fire, the man asked for a blanket.

"Ain't got a spare. You'll just have to make do with your duster."

He yammered on for a while. Finally, I cocked my Peacemaker. "One more word and I'll blow the end of your nose off. A second word will take off your right earlobe. The third, your left. So what'll it be?"

He pursed his lips and after a fashion, I holstered my pistol. "That's more like it."

I was dead-dog tired. My legs ached from three hours in the saddle, and my brain ached from all the thinking—how to pack, how to cook over a campfire. Hell, how to build a fire. I didn't have to do none of those things when I lived at the Tasty Chicken, or at the livery, either. At least I knew how to boil coffee.

Once the night settled in, I settled into my bedroll. It

wasn't as comfortable as a feather bed, for sure. First a rock poked my butt, then a stick poked my back. It took a considerable amount of wiggling and scooching around to get comfortable, but as tired as I was, sleep came easy.

Until the coyotes started howling. Or maybe it was the wolves. Sorta made a body wonder if they was fixin' to have me for supper. I held real still as the howling sliced over me, first one way, then the other. I felt a little sheepish for being such a coward. Pa slept out all the time and never thought a thing about it.

Then a twig snapped and I sat straight up in my bedroll, peering wide-eyed into the dark. The stranger was tipped over and sawing logs, so it hadn't been him making that noise. Besides, the twig had snapped on my other side.

A white wispy form in the shape of a horse floated from the creek to the bush not far from camp. I must've gone loco for imagining such a sight, and then I saw a white wispy man astride the horse. Was I awake or asleep?

I shook my head and blinked my eyes, but sure enough, this three-legged horse walked right into camp as if he wasn't missing a leg at all. The rider took off his hat and grinned at me.

"Howdy, Honey. Roscoe Peevey at your service, ma'am."

Damnation! It was that same voice I'd been hearing for the last few months—the one that told me which Walton brother to watch first, and all those other things. I must've been daft as a two-headed goat.

"Who the hell are you?"

"I told you. Of course, you might know me as Texas Lightning."

He stepped off his horse—actually, he more floated off his horse—and came toward me. His legs moved as if he was walking but his feet went right through any rocks or brush in the way. I'd never seen anything so strange—in fact, I wasn't so sure I was seeing it now. Sure enough, I had to be screwy as a pig's tail.

"Stay right where you are, mister." First I'd been hearing things and now I was seeing things. Maybe the sun had baked my head. Next town I came to, I'd have to check into getting a new hat.

"Don't be scared, Honey. I'm a spirit. You folks call us ghosts, but we don't haunt nothing or no one, we're just here to help folks out, and I've been sent to help you."

Shit, oh dear. Crazed as a buffalo bull in rut. Plumb roostered without even drinking any bug juice.

"I don't want no help. Go away." There I was, talking to thin air—yelling, more like it. If that don't beat all. I sure wouldn't be telling the folks back home about this.

The mule-thieving stranger snorted a couple times. "A man's trying to get some sleep over here."

"Just you never mind." I thought about asking if he'd seen the spirit named Roscoe, too, but then he might think I was a spoke short of a wheel. I wasn't so sure but what he would be right.

The ghost hovered near, sending a chill down my spine. "Have you thought of what you're going to do with this fellow you caught?"

"Turn him loose, I guess." I made sure my voice was low so the stranger's snoring was louder than my words.

"Best you take his boots and weapons, else he's liable to do you in, and out here, he'd get away with it."

"I already ran off his horse."

"I saw that, poor thing—he's about to come over to the spirit side. He ain't old enough, but years of hard handling takes a toll on a body, whether man or beast."

"Maybe he'll find a wild horse herd that will take him in and he can live his last days free." Was I really talking to a danged ghost? I must be loony as a shaved skunk in a snowstorm.

"Sleep now. I'll be on my way—might let you see me tomorrow."

"Let me see you?"

"Yep. You can see me—your prisoner friend can't. I decide. Now, go to sleep." He disappeared into the night.

Right. Sleep—as if I didn't have enough to think about. Did ghosts even exist? Either that one did, or I was kookier than a drunk goose.

But I was danged tired. My whole life had changed, I had my first prisoner—not that I wanted him—and spent the afternoon in the saddle, which was wearing in itself. It didn't take long before the stranger's gentle snoring put me to sleep, even though the coyotes started howling again.

The next morning, the first rays of the sun brought the bird's songs. What a pleasant way to wake up. Now I knew what Papa meant when he'd said he was happiest on the trail.

My prisoner still snored like an old bear with his nose stuck in a beehive. Rather than wake him up, I tended to my chores—best they get done before he woke up and started whining again. Besides, all this packing business was new to me and I needed to get everything put back together again. We had a big day ahead of us.

Sassy and Pickles trotted into camp as soon as I opened the oat bag. I gave Sassy a handful and Pickles two, then patted him on the rump and commenced to currying the both of them.

Wheat had warned me that a dirty animal would get galled, and those sores are hard to heal. Not only that, but you can't use the beast while they're mending, for the sores would be right where the cinch goes. So no matter how big of a hurry I was in, the donkey and the mule had to be clean as a blushing bride's cheeks before I saddled them.

"I'd hold real still if I was you." The stranger's voice sounded menacing and I froze right where I was.

Chapter 19

Hurt My Toe

Since I hadn't turned around yet, I didn't know if the dirty vulture held a pistol on me or not. My fingers itched to yank the rifle around and blast him to kingdom come—except it was in the scabbard. Wakum had told me that I should learn to throw a knife but I wasn't interested at the time. Sure would've been a handy skill right now.

"Go on and leave me alone, mister. Stickin' your nose in my camp was your idea, not mine."

"You run off my horse. I reckon that mule's a fair trade."

"My mule is worth ten of your horses." One quick glance around and I saw he held a derringer on me. Lesson learned—search prisoners better. I wondered if he'd had another knife hidden, too. Elsewise, how could he have untied himself?

"Could be, but I'm taking him, and if you report me, I'll report you for horse thievin'."

"Suit yourself." This would be fun to watch. My bet was that he wouldn't stay in the saddle more than about fifteen seconds—and that was if he could ride good. Pickles had several tricks that would deposit a rider in the dirt in a hurry. I turned to face the stranger and said, "I'll saddle him for you. He's a mite particular."

"I'll give him a sound whoopin' before I get on.

That'll fix his hide."

I kept quiet. He'd find out soon enough that no man beats an animal of mine. Or any animal if I could help it. Only thing was, how to keep him from doing it hadn't come to me yet.

"Well, don't just stand there." He waved his derringer toward Pickles. "Get that mule saddled. I want two canteens full of water and your food while you're at it. Might just take this donkey—could get twenty bucks for her in Cheyenne."

My gunbelt was under the saddle where the night dampness wouldn't get to my Peacemakers. They was loaded and ready to go, and I was ready to use them. I sidestepped toward the saddle, not taking my eyes off the sidewinder who was bent on stealing my animals. Whether he'd shoot me or not, I didn't know. He seemed to be more of a thief than a murderer, but a body couldn't tell, considering how he'd treated his horse.

Pickles had never once pitched a hissy when I'd saddled him, and I hoped he wouldn't now, on account of I needed to be able to fire a clear shot without worrying about hitting my mule—if I got a chance.

Wakum could've told me about this sort of thing. He'd know what to do—Wheat, too. I didn't, so I reckoned my best chance would be to wait until the owlhoot made a mistake. Then I'd either shoot him or whomp the tonsils out of him through his asshole, whichever was handier. In fact, I'd whomp him twice just for scaring me half out of my wits. And for the inconvenience.

"Come on, lady. Move it."

I wasn't in no hurry, so he just gave me ammunition. I

patted Pickles on the neck. Sassy trotted up for her petting, too. When I commenced to brushing Pickles, the stranger huffed.

"Hell and damnation, woman! Put the saddle on."

"You don't want the mule to get galled, do you?" I asked, not missing a stroke. "Won't do you much good if he can't carry you. A brushing only takes five minutes."

He glared at me. "Make it quick."

I kept up a steady pace, brushing Pickles the same way I always did. Of course, my innards churned with every stroke but the nasty old buzzard didn't need to know that.

After a few minutes, he said, "That's damn well enough brushing. Now get on with it."

"Got to pick his hooves."

"No, you don't."

"Yes, sir. This ain't my mule, and the owner wouldn't be too happy to get him back lame."

"He ain't getting it back, so saddle the son of a bitch. Now."

By the way the man was waggling that derringer around, I reckoned he was getting a mite impatient. I wanted to push him a little more, but not at the risk of a bullet in my back—not even from a peashooter.

"Don't say I didn't warn you." I picked up the saddle blanket and set it real careful-like on Pickles's back. Then I scooted it up half an inch, then back an inch, then up an inch—all the while planning on how I'd draw my Peacemaker from under the saddle and take care of the dirty bastard.

"Quit fiddling with that blanket and get the saddle on."

I bent over and lifted the far edge of the saddle until I

could see my pistols, when Sassy nuzzled my arm, wanting a pet. "Go chase off the bastard, girl," I muttered in her ear.

One Peacemaker had the grip sticking out to where I could grab it. To the stranger, I said, "I'm thinkin' you might want a cup of coffee before you ride out."

Bless her heart, Sassy ran behind him just like I wanted her to, and nipped him on the butt hard enough to tear his britches. Then she ran off into the trees, bucking and braying.

He spun around to take a shot at her and that was my chance. I grabbed my pistol, cocked it as I aimed, and fired at his derringer. His pistol flew ten feet and blood squirted out of his hand. He howled like a coyote with his tail on fire, grabbed his wounded hand with the other, and stuck both between his bent legs. I ran over and gave him a swift kick in the jaw, hard as I could, which hurt my toe even through my new boot, and he took a nice little nap.

I found my rope that I'd tied him up with the night before and sure enough, he'd cut it. So I commenced to stripping off his boots and every stitch of his clothes, which wasn't easy, considering the scoundrel was out cold. In one leg of his britches, I found a nice pearl-handled Bowie knife, which seemed to want to be mine, so I kept it. Call it a service fee.

Once he was good and tied up, I commenced with my morning chores. Just because he'd caused a ruckus wasn't no reason why I shouldn't have breakfast. Besides, he'd made me a mite skittish and I needed to settle my feathers some.

After I got the fire going good, I put on a pot of coffee

to boil and threw a couple strips of bacon in the frying pan. I reckoned the stranger would wake up hungry but he'd put me all out of the mood to share. He wasn't even gonna get any beans.

Along about that time, he started to stir and groan. I ignored the bottom-feeder and ate my breakfast. After all, he hadn't made the start of my day very pleasant. Then again, I paid him back in kind.

"Stickers is poking in my back," he whimpered. "Are you gonna find a doctor for my hand?"

"I expect once you walk back to the town, you can see the doctor yourself."

"Where's my clothes?"

"Packed on Sassy. I'll leave them half a mile down the road and you can pick them up there."

"When are you going to untie me?"

"When I damned well feel like it. I ain't in too good of humor right now, so shut your pie hole."

I took my time doing the rest of the morning chores, gave Pickles his pickle, and mounted up. Sassy didn't need no lead rope on account of she stuck by me whether I wanted her to or not, so I didn't see any reason to tie one on her. We headed down the road and crossed the creek, which took us a goodly distance from the nekkid tied-up mule thief.

Looked like a good camping spot, although I didn't need one, so I dumped off his clothes and boots. On second thought, I left him his derringer on account of no man was safe out here without some protection, but I kept his two knives and other weapons. I reckoned he'd have himself untied and be on his way by now, for I'd loosened the knots before I left.

It still irked me to lose a perfectly good rope, even if he'd cut it into a few pieces. The danged thing wasn't even paid for yet. Nor anything else, which was why I didn't dawdle.

My legs and butt was sore and getting sorer by the minute. When I dismounted at noon, I was as spraddle-legged as a two-bit whore at a bachelor party.

"You done good this morning, Honey."

I jumped at the ghost's voice. "Roscoe, don't go sneakin' up on me like that."

"I been right beside you all along."

"If that's the case, I could've used a little help earlier."

"Didn't see where you needed none."

"How come can't I see you?"

"Harder in the daytime. If you look close, you can see me when we ride by a big bush with a shadow."

"We ain't riding right now, and besides, there ain't no shadows at noon."

"You'll just have to wait, then."

"So are you dogging me all the time?"

"Mostly. 'Ceptin' when I'm not."

"That's helpful." Then again, I didn't know what good a ghost would be anyhow.

Sassy and Pickles wanted a drink, so I let them swill their fill before loosening their cinches. They didn't seem bothered by having a ghost and his horse around.

As for me, walking around helped ease the stiffness of my poor sit-down. I wasn't about to unpack everything just for a cup of coffee, so I drank from the creek, washed my face, filled all the canteens, and then chewed on some jerky from the Golden Ruhl. Thad had sent two pounds of the stuff, which ought to keep me fed for a week if I was careful.

Of course, I hoped to have Roxbury locked up and two hundred dollars in my wallet before a week was up.

Roscoe—that's the ghost, remember—didn't say nothing the rest of the hour we was stopped so I didn't know whether he'd stuck around or not. He'd make himself known when he wanted to. Meantime, I had to remember to be careful not to talk to him when anyone was within earshot, lest they think I was tetched. They'd be right.

About the time I swallowed my jerky, I spotted the stranger's horse—reins trailing and saddle askew.

"Come on, Pickles. Let's go get that poor horse unsaddled."

I tightened the cinch and mounted up. Five seconds later, I was eating dirt. "You could've found a spot with no rocks." I picked the gravel out of my cheek and got a pickle out of the bag. The mule gobbled it down and off we went.

The horse spotted us but didn't run. Being so gaunt, he likely didn't have a whole helluva lot of wind. He seemed to take right to Pickles, and Sassy nipped his butt—jealous, it looked like. She had no reason to be on account of Pickles didn't pay the gelding no mind, and besides we wouldn't be taking him with us.

His bridle had rubbed a sore spot in his mouth and the saddle had rubbed sores on his withers. I felt sorry for the poor beast—he'd deserved better. I brushed him down good and put some salve that Wheat had given me on the sores.

"All right, boy." I patted him on the butt. "Go find yourself some friends. There's bound to be a herd of mustangs around close."

He wouldn't leave so I hissed at him and slapped my leg. That scared him some and he jumped back, but he wouldn't go. The last thing I wanted was to be stuck with another man's horse, especially that man was likely to claim I stole it.

After thinking a spell, I dumped out a cup of oats, which got his attention right away. I jumped on Pickles. "Let's go!"

There I was, in the dirt again. I forgot to give him his pickle. This was getting damned old.

Chapter 20

My Chicks Didn't Match

The stranger's gelding scarfed up all the oats before Pickles could eat one pickle, for the poor beast was half starved. I swear that horse smiled, and stuck right by Pickles' side. Sassy got contrary and horned in between them, so close that she mashed my foot in the stirrup. No doubt about it, the horse planned to go with us.

Which made me a horse thief. I didn't know what to do—couldn't tie him up, and he needed some healing and tending. So I made up my mind to let him come along until we got to the next town, where I'd leave him at the livery, then explain to the owner what had happened and pay board for a week.

The slimy buzzard ought to make it to town in a couple days, and he could claim his horse then. He didn't deserve that sweet of a horse, but that wasn't for me to say.

As the day wore on, my butt wore out. My inner thighs felt like Mexican hot sauce that one of Mama's cooks liked to make. If it didn't burn going in and coming out, she said it wasn't hot enough. I expect this riding business wouldn't be so bad once I got used to it. But right then, I was ready to take a soak in a steaming hot tub. If such a thing could be found in the out and beyond.

I missed Mama, and I sure missed the bathtub. I tried my best to ride into the wind so I didn't have to smell myself.

Pa had said living on the trail took grit. He didn't say I'd have grit all over, including under my begonias. I didn't have much up front but I'd wrapped a cloth strip around my ribcage to keep what bosom I had from flopping, and also to keep my shirt from rubbing. That had been a good idea and actually worked.

The butt and legs—no. I pulled Pickles to a stop, got off real slow, and just stood there a minute. "How about I walk for a spell?"

Pickles wiggled one ear. My guess is he didn't much care one way or the other. I walked alongside for maybe a mile and then my feet started hurting, too, so I got back on. This time, I didn't forget to feed Pickles his pickle.

The gelding looked happy as can be, tossing his head and kicking up his heels as if to tell me he still had some life in him.

We followed the road—more of a game trail—up hills and down hills. I swear, there wasn't five feet of flat ground to be found. Nor a human. Whether we were on Roxbury's trail, I had no idea. My only choice was to keep going and that's what we did.

A mile or so farther down the road, a man called. I reckoned it was just that damned ghost again so I ignored him. Then I saw a fellow dressed only in his longjohns.

"Howdy! Can you help me?"

The tall wiry man had no shoes on and his feet were scratched and bleeding. I reckoned him to be near his fortieth year by the looks of his weathered skin and the wrinkles around his eyes. Those wrinkles showed that he'd laughed a lot and I read him to be a decent sort with a good sense of humor in normal times. Which this wasn't.

"What happened to your boots, mister?"

"A weasel took them, and everything else, too." He scrubbed his graying stubble, which contrasted with his dark brown hair. "All my money, my guns—everything."

"Do you know who it was?"

"You're a woman!"

"Last time I looked. Who done this to you?"

"A bunko man, near as I can tell." The man sagged onto a rock, puffed out his cheeks, and blew as if he was trying to blow his bad luck away. "He sold me a fake goldmine claim, then when he took me out to see what it was I bought, he walloped me in the head. I don't know how long I was out, but when I woke up, I couldn't remember where I was or nothing. He took off with everything."

"He call himself Ed Roxbury?"

"How'd you know?"

"Just a sneakin' hunch. I'm after him, so if you'll tell me which way he went, I'd be obliged."

"Have no idea a'tall." He rubbed the back of his head. "Like I said, he knocked me out, cold as a winterkill steer."

"You hungry?"

"Starved. Haven't had a bite for nearly two days, and then all I had was a piece of jerky. The bastard—er, excuse me, ma'am—even took my last piece."

"You stay set and I'll fetch you some beans and jerky. Can't make coffee until we get to a stream."

"Thank you, ma'am."

I had to shove the gelding out of the way to get to Sassy. Luckily, the food was on top so I didn't have to take her pack off. When I got back and handed him the food, he wolfed it down like he hadn't had a thing to eat for a month.

"If there's a town around here where I can buy supplies, I can let you have more beans."

"How about you come to my place. The wife can fix you a nice meal and you can sleep over, too, if you want."

"I'm after Roxbury and I don't want him to get too far ahead."

"I can see that, but you've got to eat and sleep. My place is only ten miles or so from here. I'm Bruce Yates. My wife and me ain't rich, but we could give you a hot, tasty supper and a good night's rest."

"Honey Beaulieu, and I take you up on your offer."

"Beaulieu? I know a man who goes by Beaulieu. Said most folks call him 'Blue.' He always stops by—even pays for his meal."

"That's my pa."

"Good man." He eyed the gelding. "Mind if I ride your horse? I'm plumb wore out."

"Ain't got any tack, but if you can sit him, you can ride him. He ain't mine, though." I told him what had happened.

"I thought that horse looked familiar. The feller you're talking about stopped by five or six days ago—I don't rightly have my timing." Yates touched the back of his head, likely where he got bonked. "We fed him, let him sleep in the barn, and damned if he didn't steal a weaner pig when he rode out. I saw what was left of the pig at some cold campfire ashes not far from here."

"You see everyone who comes through this way?"

"Pert near. We live right off the main road—only homestead within thirty miles."

"All right, let's head out. You can use Sassy's lead rope for a hackamore—the gelding sticks pretty close to us, so I don't think you'll have a bit of trouble with him."

* * *

A little more than an hour later, we rode into Yates's barnyard. His wife, dressed in green calico with no bonnet on her brown braids, busted out of the house and ran toward him. Chickens squawked and scattered every which way. A brown dog nosed his way in front of her, but she pulled him aside.

"Bruce!" she called when we was still thirty feet away. "I was so worried. I thought—"

His face lit up like the first sunrays after a heavy rain. "I'm here, darlin'. Everything's all right," he hollered back. To me, he said quietly, "That's my wife, Charlotte. She's a sweet thing, and I don't think she'll be put off by you wearing britches and all."

When we reined up in front of the house, I thought Charlotte was gonna jump on the horse and smother her husband. Instead, Yates slid off and gave his wife a big bear hug and a long, long kiss. She seemed awful familiar. I had to think on it for a while.

After Yates came up for air but without letting go of his wife, he tilted his head in the direction of the barn. "You can settle your animals anytime." Then he went back to lovin' all over Charlotte. They must be newlyweds.

I reckoned they needed a little time alone, so I dismounted and headed to the water trough with all three animals following. I felt like a mother hen sometimes.

Only my chicks didn't match. And I hoped the gelding would realize that he wasn't mine. I already had a mule and a donkey—more than enough, considering I didn't have a reason to own no animals just a few months ago.

After the animals drank their fill, I set to removing the load from Sassy, unsaddling Pickles, and currying the both of them and the gelding. By then, Yates called me to the house. I washed up as best I could so's not to stink up the place, and headed in.

"We'll have supper in about forty-five minutes, so just make yourself to home." Charlotte was at the stove fixing a big meal—beef, potatoes, gravy, and some sort of greens. "I thank you so much for bringing Bruce home to me."

Her husband sat in a kitchen chair dressed in clean work clothes, with his hand resting on the handle of a coffee mug, and his gaze locked on his wife's backside. I made a note to make myself scarce as soon as we ate supper.

"You sit wherever you please," Charlotte said after her husband had made the introductions. "The couch is comfortable or you can sit at the kitchen table."

"The couch looks nice and soft." I headed for it, and sure enough, when I sat, it nearly swallowed me up.

The house fascinated me. I hadn't been in a house more than two or three times in my whole life since I'd always lived in a whorehouse, and the school kids didn't exactly welcome me into their homes. The small kitchen had a stove, dry sink, a counter, and a pie safe. Looked like she used the kitchen table for rolling out dough and such.

The rest of the room had a couch, a rocker, and beside the rocker, a big bag of sewing stuff. Then there was a doorway, which I reckoned led to their bedroom. Overall, it looked like a cozy little place and certainly the couple enjoyed their home.

Still, Charlotte's likeness niggled at me but I couldn't place her. Maybe I had gone to school with her. She had to be within a year or two of my age.

Yates took a drink of coffee and said to his wife, "Honey is Devlin Beaulieu's daughter."

She cast a haunted glance my way. Yup, we had run across one another at some time—and it most likely was at the Tasty Chicken. Charlotte would undoubtedly want to keep that quiet so I wouldn't mention it, and besides, I still couldn't quite place her.

"There's a newspaper there if you want to read it, Honey," Charlotte called. "It's a couple months old but you might find something interesting in it."

She had to be acquainted with me, elsewise she'd have called me 'Miss Beaulieu.' But everyone in Fry Pan Gulch called me by my first name—mostly that was customers and whores in the Tasty Chicken, for the respectable townsfolk generally ignored me. Until I took the deputy job, I didn't know many of the town citizens unless they frequented the whorehouse.

But it didn't much matter. I'd be there for a meal and a roof over my head, even if it was a barn, and then I'd be on my way. Roxbury wouldn't be standing in one spot waiting for me to arrest him. Meantime, the flavorsome aroma of roast beef was calling my name and my mouth watered.

I picked up the paper and scanned the front page. "Might be something about Roxbury in here."

"She's after him," Yates said to his wife. "Says there's a bounty on him."

Unless they had clues for me, I wasn't interested in talking about my plans—the less people knew, the better. When hooves clomped on the front porch, I didn't have to say no more, for Sassy had come calling. I put the old newspaper aside and extricated myself from the man-eating couch that wanted to keep me right where I'd sat, and headed outside.

"My apologies, ma'am," I said as I passed Charlotte, who was forking beef onto a platter. "Sassy gets lonesome, and she ain't never figured out that donkeys don't belong in the house."

Charlotte tossed the fork into the sink. "I'll come help you while Bruce washes up. Supper's about ready."

"I already washed." Bruce sniffed his armpit. "Might take a bath later, though."

"We'll be right back," Charlotte said. "I need to get some fresh air."

Once outside, she turned to me, her face drawn and a tear in her eye. She whispered, "I know Ed Roxbury."

Chapter 21

It's What You Don't See

I coaxed Sassy off the porch and headed to the barn, knowing that the donkey would follow, and gestured to Charlotte for her to come along, too. Once we got out of earshot of the house, I stopped and patted Sassy as she rubbed her head on my chest.

"I wish he'd never come here." Charlotte spoke of Roxbury with a tear in her eye.

"Your husband doesn't know that you know Roxbury, I bet."

She looked at the ground and shook her head. "I never told him."

"Why are you telling me?"

"Because maybe I can help you find him. He was big on bragging while Bruce was out doing chores."

I wondered if Roxbury still had Marshal Fripp's horse. "Did he ride a big bay with a blaze?"

"Yes. Why you ask?"

"Because he stole that horse from the Fry Pan Gulch town marshal, and Fripp—that's the marshal—is after him, too. Not only that, the U.S. deputy marshal is along for the ride. One way or the other, one of us will catch him. So which way was Roxbury headed when he left your husband for dead?"

"Rawlins. Said he had some mining claims from Wind

River that he can sell to men who came there expecting to strike it rich."

"There ain't no gold rush going on now. Besides, he was headed toward Cheyenne." If what she said was true, I'd been riding the wrong direction since the minute I left Fry Pan Gulch.

"Pa said—"

"Pa? Roxbury's your pa?" Could be that she wanted me to chase off in the wrong direction, so I had to know if he really went to Rawlins, or if she was throwin' a horse apple to see if I'd fetch it.

"I'm afraid so." She dragged the toe of her shoe through the dirt. "It ain't nothing I'm proud of."

Now that I knew her upbringing wasn't a respectable sort, I had to ask, "Did you work at the Tasty Chicken?"

"Why would you think that?"

"Because I know I've seen you somewhere before, and my mama owns the Tasty Chicken—I grew up there. Women came and women left. Some ended up dead and some ended up married, but I always hoped that the women who'd gone had found a happy life, and it looks to me like you did with Bruce."

"Yes, I worked in Denver for a year and then a man said he wanted to marry me so I went with him, but he dumped me in Fry Pan Gulch and I had to eat, so I ended up working in the Tasty Chicken. Your mama was real nice to me and didn't put up any fuss at all when I told her I was leaving."

"So you met Yates there?"

"No, I met him in the Golden Ruhl store. He was buying supplies for his homestead and said he needed a wife. I said I needed a husband and he said, 'Well then, let's get married.' So we did. That was two years ago. I'd only worked at the Tasty Chicken for a few weeks so I wasn't known in town. Mayor Tench married us and Bruce took me out here the next day. We've been happy ever since and will be as long as Pa doesn't mess everything up. But he always does."

"Your husband won't hear a word about your past from me, just so you know."

"I thank you for that. I started to tell him once but he said he didn't want to know, and I understand. Some things are best left unsaid."

"When I turn in your pa, they'll send him to the slammer for a long time." Could even hang, what with him being a horse thief. Folks in this part of the country didn't have no sense of humor whatsoever when it came to stealing horses. But I kept mum about the possibility.

She frowned and pursed her lips. "He was never a decent father to me, nor a good husband to my mama. She died on account of him not being there to help her. I won't go into it now but trust me, I ain't beholden to him in any manner. Only to Bruce. He's a wonderful man and deserves the best I can give him. Pa only causes harm—never good. It's best he's where he can't hurt innocent people."

"I'm sorry he put you in such a bad way, Charlotte."

"And now," she rested her palm on her belly, "Bruce and me, we're starting a family. I want my baby to be safe."

Well, damn, that was two babes that depended on me catching Roxbury—Emma's and now Charlotte's. Seemed as if there was a dreadful lot of young 'uns about to be born, and none of them needed the likes of Roxbury around. On the other hand, I did need that two hundred and fifty bucks.

"I'll do my best to get him out of your way."

"Let's eat supper, then." She grabbed my arm and walked with me as if we'd been best friends since we was little. "I fixed a fine meal—nothing fancy but it'll fill you up. And I'll cook extra for breakfast so you can have some vittles for the road."

"I'm obliged. Thanks."

Yates did smell better when we got into the house, so he must've washed up while we was outside palavering.

"I'm ready for some good food," he said as he seated his wife. He'd already dished up the food. Good man.

He started praying just about as I was gonna stab a biscuit. I pulled my hand back and acted like I had a hitch in my shoulder, then bowed my head like I'd seen folks do at the prayer meetings they used to have in the town square, which was actually three-sided on account of the creek.

The meal tasted wonderful but I nearly fell asleep in my chair. Yates gave me a cup of coffee while Charlotte rustled up some blankets and a pillow.

"You can sleep wherever you want—the living room or the barn," she said as she handed the bundle of bedding to me. "Suit yourself."

"The barn's best—I can keep an eye on the animals and my supplies." Now that I knew Roxbury was Charlotte's pa, I expected he might come back and if he did, I'd be ready for him. Also, I didn't want to put a woman who was with child in a dangerous situation.

"I'll go help you get your bed set up." Charlotte picked up the lantern. "You'll need this shortly, especially if you read before you go to sleep."

When we got to the barn, she hung the lantern on a nail by the door.

"I can make my own bed—you don't have to help. Get in the house and take care of that poor husband of yours. He missed you sorely."

"I have one more thing to tell you that I remembered during supper. Pa told me he took on a new partner."

"So I'm looking for two men. Did you see the other one?"

"No, he planned to meet him in Rawlins. But I remember his name if that helps."

"It surely does."

"Clem Walton."

* * *

It took some doing, but the gelding finally stayed with Bruce Yates. Two days in the saddle and my butt was finally getting used to riding, but not without a few pains here and there. Next town I came to, a little whiskey might help.

"Looks like you'll get two for one."

I jerked in the saddle, which didn't make Pickles too happy. It was that damned ghost talking to me again. He'd pestered me the entire two days since I'd left the Yates ranch. About the time I thought he would leave me alone, he popped up again.

"Don't go sneaking up on me like that, Roscoe."

"I'm a ghost, remember? It happens."

"You could at least let me know you're there before

you start yammering at me."

"Hard to do in the daytime."

I looked around but couldn't see him, or even a wavy spot. "I'm only after Roxbury and that two hundred and fifty dollars. Clem's a murderer, all right, but I don't know if he has a bounty on him yet."

"Want I should scout ahead for you?"

"Charlotte said he'd be in Rawlins. Ain't much to do until I get there and ask around."

"Nope, she said he was headed there to meet Walton. She didn't say he'd *be* there."

"Aw c'mon, Roscoe. It's the same thing."

"You're a smart gal, Honey, and you've seen a lot in your twenty-two years—more than most. But you're a greenhorn when it comes to hunting men. You'll learn."

"That ain't news. I admit to being a greenhorn at a lot of things—riding mules, packing donkeys, building campfires, tracking men, sleeping in someone's barn. Just about every minute since I left Fry Pan Gulch, I done something I ain't never done before."

"What's over the hill ahead?"

"How in the ever-lovin' tarnation should I know that?"

"By what you see. Then again it's what you don't see."

"I see a hill that looks the same as the last dozen I passed."

"You see blue sky—no smoke, no birds flying willy-nilly, no dust. That means no one's camped over there. Unless they camped cold and are holdin' real still just waiting for you. And you don't even have your Peacemakers at the ready."

I moved my pistol to where I could pull in a hurry, but then my skin crawled some. "Have you been up there?"

"Nope. Just telling you what you ought to be looking at. Then there's the hearing. Heard any nickers? Hollering? Birds chirping?"

That embarrassed me some on account of I had to admit I'd been woolgathering for the last several miles and paid no nevermind to any such goin's on.

"Roscoe?"

"Yeah?"

"How come you're dead?"

"Because I didn't pay respects to the sign. You got to ride along as if someone's set on beefing you beyond every hill and around every bend."

"That don't sound too fun."

"You ain't caught anyone yet, so you ain't pissed no one off. But if you're any good at manhunting, the time will come when you'll have to watch your back as much as your front."

I doubted I'd be hunting bounties for long, but expect that the ghost was right on that count. Papa had said much the same.

"Did you ever hunt for bounties?"

"Naw, they was after me. Never caught me, though."

Roscoe still hadn't told me what done him in. I halfway wondered if Pa killed him, but Pa wasn't a killer. He's the one who told me where to shoot a man to keep him from doing more harm, but not kill him.

After another hour and passing a few roostered-up soldiers, I did see smoke on the horizon—likely a saloon or a whorehouse. My gut told me we was getting near

Roxbury, or Clem, or both. It'd suit me fine if Clem had gone off somewhere else, but near as I knew, he'd never been on his own, so I reckoned he'd want to partner up. As for Roxbury, I had the impression that he generally worked solo.

Pickles kept nosing the canteen that Sassy carried, so I dismounted and poured a little water in my hat while he drank. After I did the same for Sassy, I drank my fill, which emptied the canteen. We still had two canteens on Sassy and the canteen I carried on Pickles was mostly full. Even so, I'd have been a lot more at ease if I knew where to find a creek.

I put the wet hat back on my head and found out that cooled me off—a comfort to remember for other hot days. And my aching butt reminded me to feed a pickle to the mule so we didn't have no snags when I got back on. My legs felt a little better than the day before, but still stiff.

"Let's go see what's over yonder." I reined Pickles to the left onto a wagon trail that looked promising. It only made sense that someone would make camp by a creek or a pond. "Maybe this'll take us there, and with a little luck, we'll find ourselves some water."

With even more luck, Roxbury would be there and we could go home.

Chapter 22

Another Four Bits

While I enjoyed open country, downright magnificent in its own wild and harsh way, I couldn't say the same for dirty hair. Next time I took off on a hunt, I'd tie a bandana on my head like Mama's housekeeper did. That'd keep some of the dirt out.

The bigger the country, the smaller I felt, and lonesome, too. The ghost didn't even bother to come around to keep me company. At least a few travelers, mostly soldiers, greeted me as they passed. The closer I got to the smoke, the drunker those soldiers got. Sure enough, the tall smoke thread had to have come from a chimney, not a campfire.

Where Roscoe went, I had no blasted idea, but as we neared the smoke, my innards told me to be at the ready. A body would think that a ghost would come in handy at times like these. Then again, this ghost seemed to like to talk and not a lot else. So much for helping.

I slipped a knife in my boot, got both Peacemakers within quick drawing position, and unbuckled the strap on the rifle scabbard.

The trail crossed the railroad track, and dang if it wasn't a trial getting Pickles to cross the thing. He must have thought it was a couple of long iron snakes or something, what with the fuss he put up.

First he tossed his head back and nearly hit me on the nose. Then he bunny-hopped a spell. I pulled leather and managed to stay on during his shenanigans, but I dropped a pistol. Sassy crossed back and forth over the tracks about six times while Pickles was making up his mind to do what I asked of him. Finally, I dismounted and fetched my Peacemaker, got a bread and butter pickle, then walked to the other side of the tracks. If he wanted a pickle, he'd have to come get it.

His ears drooped and he pawed the dirt, but finally he bunched up on his haunches and jumped across. It was the damnedest thing I ever did see. I had no idea he could jump like that. Anyway, I gave him his bread and butter pickle, mounted up, and off we went to see what was over the next hill, and whether or not there was water to be had.

Or trouble.

Roxbury shouldn't be too hard to find—I knew all of his names that he used and he cut a wide swath wherever he went, what with him cheating folks and all. Add Clem and his skull filled with man-seed instead of brains, and I reckoned anyone could find them, even me.

I wasn't about to go over that rise without cleaning my shootin' iron, especially since Roxbury, with or without Clem, could be in this neck of the woods. How he reckoned he'd dupe folks here was anyone's guess—it didn't look none too prosperous to me. All I saw was rolling hills, an occasional cow skull, brush and grass, with a few trees dotting the land.

Occasionally, a coyote or a jackrabbit ran off when we came too close to their hiding places. Several herds of pronghorn ran—leaping as if they had wings—over the hills. I loved to watch them.

That's when Pickles got skitterish and didn't want to go any farther. He hopped around a bit—maybe he seen a snake or something. I let him work out his worries—just sat on him until he decided to go again.

A couple drunken soldiers met me just as Pickles finally settled down, but we still wasn't going anywhere.

"Howdy," one of them slurred. He lopped over his horse and I expected he would fall off anytime. "Careful of the whiskey over yon."

"I'll take heed."

"Damn, you're a woman!" the other one said. He looked considerably more alert, although he could use a bath, a shave, and his clothes needed a good brushing. "I'm Martin and this here's Emmett."

I nodded, not about to say my name or even that it was nice to meet them, on account of it wasn't. "Best be on my way."

"Maybe we could have a little fun right here," Martin said.

I pulled. "Maybe not." Then I cocked the Peacemaker. "You seen an old man with a gray beard at the saloon?"

"Hold on, gal. I meant no harm." He raised both hands, still holding the reins in his left. "Ain't a saloon—it's a hog ranch."

I'd heard about hog ranches, mostly that they was dreary places where whores went to work until they died. Whoring was a profession where a gal started at the top and worked her way down, lest she had business sense like Mama. Most didn't.

"Seen the man I asked you about?"

"Wasn't looking at men, if you know what I mean."

"Heard any women hollering?" I lowered my weapon.

"I make 'em holler at every time."

The disheveled soldier wasn't going to tell me anything so I let it drop. "Be on your way, then."

Emmett headed down the road but Martin lowered his hands and reached for his pocket. I set bead on him again. "Careful."

"I'm just fetching my flask—don't get your dander up."

This man pissed me off but I had no truck with him and he was wasting my time. "You get on down the road. Right now. I'll be keeping an eye on you until you're out of sight."

That did two things—got rid of the soldiers, and gave Pickles more time to decide he wanted to start walking. Occasionally, mules could be a genuine tribulation.

Sassy had gone off the road a ways to graze during all the delay. Once Pickles decided to move, I whistled at her and she came trotting back. It didn't take long to get to the hog ranch.

Out front, by the well, a half-dressed woman stood in what she must've thought was a *come hither* pose, her weight on one leg and the other akimbo, and her scrawny hip jutted out. Her face was drawn and she had a sore on the side of her mouth. I felt sorrier for her than she could ever know. Also, I was grateful that she was downwind.

"Howdy," she greeted. "I'm happy to show you a little fun."

"No thanks," I said as I dismounted. Three horses

stood tied to the hitching post in front of the log and mud shack. One was a cavalry horse, one had a W branded on the left shoulder. Without knowing the Walton brand, and I could've kicked myself for not paying attention, I couldn't be sure if it was Clem's or not. But the third was Fripp's horse—that I knew for certain.

Wouldn't you know, the first whorehouse I came to, and there was my prey. Easy money. And I'd get Fripp's horse back, too. Not that I much gave a shit about him, but no one deserved to have their horse stolen.

"Oh, you're a woman. We generally only do men, but one of the girls might take you for the right price."

"Got a feller in there that likes to beat up whores?"

"We don't talk about our gents."

"I got a buck for you if you tell me which room the old man's in." I held out a dollar.

"Ain't but one room. He's in the back left part that's curtained off." She snatched the coin and stuffed it between her begonias. "And don't you go tellin' anyone I told you."

A woman screamed and Sassy shied to where I thought she might run off.

"And Clem, the one that likes to beat up whores?"

"Right next to the other, in the back."

"How many's in there?"

"That'd be another four bits."

I gave her a couple quarters. "How many girls work here and how many men are in there?"

"The madam and two other whores. Only customers are the men you're asking about and a cavalry man, but he's passed out cold."

* * *

Whether Sassy smelled Roxbury or not, I couldn't know but she wouldn't take one step closer to the ramshackle building, and Pickles wouldn't leave Sassy. I took my rifle and a rope—Charlotte had given me one since mine was in pieces—and told them to go graze a while and meet me in fifteen minutes. I just hoped the donkey and the mule knew how to tell time.

The curtains was closed so the first thing I done was look into Roxbury's saddlebags where I found a pistol and two knives, plus over sixty dollars, which I stuffed into my vest pocket. Clem's saddlebag was full of corn whiskey. I reckoned he'd have at least a pistol on him, though. He was whoopin' it up inside with his other pistol, judging from the woman's shrieks and cries.

I headed back over to the well and put my forefinger to my lips, signaling the whore to keep her mouth shut. "The girls will get paid plenty and you'll get a little extra," I whispered, "but you have to keep quiet. You don't have to help, but stay out of the way lest you get hurt."

"Would you take me with you when you leave?"

"I can get you out of here and leave you in the next town. You'll have to ride double with Roxbury."

"We'll have to hurry, then, before Maggie starts shootin'."

"She your boss?"

The girl nodded.

"I want you to amble down the road like you was meeting a customer. When I open the door, run like hell. I'll pick you up on the way out, but don't stop running until you get to the railroad tracks. Wait there for me."

"Ain't got no shoes."

"Can't be helped—you don't have time to pack."

Truth was, my belly was plumb sour from worry, but the time had come to collect that two hundred and fifty dollars, and I aimed to get the job done.

I didn't see no other way to arrest Roxbury other than to take Clem at the same time, and that would likely involve fighting off Maggie, who'd be wanting her money. She'd get it and more, but she wouldn't know that at first.

The back wall of the house didn't have windows so I plastered my back against it and then worked my way around, ducking under the side window on account of even though the curtains was closed, I might cast a shadow. The building wasn't very big so it didn't take long to get to the door. Besides, what with all the slaps and hollering going on, they'd never hear if I snapped a twig or such. I stuffed forty dollars of Roxbury's money in the spittoon by the door.

"No!" a woman hollered. "Don't cut me!"

Clem hadn't ever cut up one of Mama's girls but that didn't mean he didn't want to. Looked like he'd taken the next step to hell, and it was time for me to stop it. As quietly as I could, I unhooked the latch. With the rifle slung over my left shoulder and a Peacemaker in each hand, I kicked in the door.

Damn if I couldn't see a thing, for my eyes were used to the bright sun and it was dark in the cabin. But they didn't need to know that. "Ladies, get out of here. Now."

The boom of a pistol in close quarters nearly deafened me, and the doorframe splintered not two inches from my ear. Luckily, my eyes adjusted in a hurry, although not completely. Clem stood at the back wall, four fresh scratches—fingernail marks—on his cheek. A woman with a fat lip and bruises all over lay on her belly on the floor, scooting away from him.

Roxbury sat up in the other cot but didn't say a word and I could see both hands, so I kept my attention on Clem. Both his guns, top and bottom, was smokin'. He aimed at me and I held bead on him.

"You have no business here, Honey," Clem growled.

"Neither do you, but you're here." Without taking my eyes off him, I told the ladies, "If you don't want to get hurt, get out of the building."

A portly woman slid a derringer from under the covers.

"Put that down, Maggie."

She cocked it. "You know my name?"

"Yep, and as you can see, I ain't a man, so I have no qualms about shooting you. Put it on the floor in front of you and kick it over here."

"Don't do it, Maggie. She'll shoot you just as she says. She shot both my brothers."

That must've made up the madam's mind because she did what I told her, then motioned for the girls to leave.

I tossed the rope to Roxbury. "Tie Clem up."

"But—"

"Do it, or I'll put so many holes in you, you'll look like a crocheted doily."

Chapter 23

You Only Get Eighty Dollars If He Dies

Clem still had his pistol pointed my direction and who knew what other weapons close at hand.

"I'm gonna kill you, Honey Beaulieu."

"Aw, that rhymes. That's mighty sweet of you. Mama was right, though—you do have a little dinky dick."

I hit the floor.

He fired over my head.

I fired and blew a nice-size chunk out of his shoulder.

The ladies was screamin' their heads off. Clem looked at his shoulder, then his knees buckled and he crumpled to the floor.

"You can tie him up now, Roxbury."

"I don't think so." He held a derringer on me. "I'm tying you up."

"Ladies," I said, "if you look in the spittoon right outside the door, you'll find forty dollars. Help me arrest this man and you can have it."

Maggie slowly reached for her own palm pistol and I nodded at her. She grabbed it, which took Roxbury's attention from me. With two strides and one swift kick, I knocked the derringer out of his hand.

"Ladies, help me tie the both of them up."

"You must want them awful bad," Maggie said.

"Two hundred and fifty dollars bad." I steadied my

pistol at Roxbury's gut. "He's wanted for horse thieving."

"How about the other one?"

"Murder, but there ain't no bounty on him yet that I know of. If he'd have been a good boy I wouldn't take him in—he ain't worth the bother."

"A woman bounty hunter?"

"Women do all kinds of things for money. In the end, I reckon we all sell our souls one way or the other."

"I reckon you're right. Speaking of money I'll go get it right now." She motioned for the other girls to tie the men up, which they seemed dreadful happy to do, especially the one who was bruised up from top to bottom. I reckoned she was the one who Clem was working over when I got there.

Only then did I notice the strong smell of sex and sweat, the dingy blankets on the bed and the mouse turds on the dirt floor. I had never seen such a sorry place in my life. Mama always kept the Tasty Chicken sparkly clean. She expected her girls to take a bath every day and wear clean clothes. The sheets were changed daily, too. I always thought that was an awful lot of unnecessary washing, but I didn't think so now.

Clem was out cold and bleeding a lot. Once the girls got Roxbury tied up real good, I asked them to help me haul Clem outside so he wouldn't bleed on their floor. To be flat truthful, I didn't want him to die—not because he didn't deserve to die, but because I didn't wanna kill no one, not even him.

"Stuff something in that hole to keep his blood in him," I told Maggie. "How far to the next town?" I hated to admit that I didn't know my way around, and I'd gone east one path and come back another.

"Fry Pan Gulch is about fifteen miles on down the tracks. Or you could go back the other way and catch the train—that's only five miles or so."

"When does the train come in?"

"In the morning."

I wasn't about to stay here until morning, especially once Maggie realized one of her whores was gone. Then I'd be bleeding on the floor. "We'll be heading to Fry Pan Gulch, then. Help me get these two fiddle-headed sidewinders on their horses."

Sassy glared at me from thirty yards off and wouldn't come into the yard. She must've still been mad at Roxbury for lashing her so bad. It stuck in my craw, too.

"It's all right, Sassy," I called. "He's tied up and he can't hurt you."

Maggie chuckled. "You sure do go on with your animals."

With a shrug, I said, "I talk the same to them as I do to people."

"They don't understand a word you say," Roxbury said.

"They understand more than most people, including you. Now, hush up."

Pickles wouldn't come over until Sassy did, but then horned in between Roxbury's horse and the donkey, as if he was making himself a barrier. I checked his cinch and fed him a bread and butter pickle. I only had two left, which worried me a mite—also worried that Clem would up and die before we got back to town.

Maggie was happy with the forty dollars, and all

smiles when she waved good-bye.

I mounted up and took the two horses' reins in my right hand, wishing I had another way to lead the horses, but a body could deal with damn near anything for fifteen miles, so I told Pickles to go home.

They must have smelled Fry Pan Gulch because both the donkey and the mule was in a bigger hurry than they'd been in since we'd left.

* * *

I swore that had to be the longest fifteen miles on this earth, what with Clem's moaning and Roxbury's bitching. My ears was more tired than my butt. Clem didn't seem any worse, although he looked a mite pale. Doc's beef tea would take care of that.

The whore's name was Dora Jean Burdett, although she said I had to call her Bessie, as that was her working name. She put up with Roxbury better than I did even though she was hanging on behind him.

"I been with lots worse," she said when I asked her how she was doing. "Long as I don't breathe through my nose, it ain't bad."

"Your legs paining you some?"

"Need to pee. Ain't used to riding, neither. Horses, anyhow."

"We'll stop ahead by those trees."

She volunteered to hold the men's hoses while they did their business, which put me to wondering how I'd deal with that if she wasn't there. Her get-around looked a bit stiff.

"Walk around some," I told her. "We'll get to Fry Pan Gulch before dark, so take your time. The animals need to drink their fill and graze a little."

I wondered what I'd do with her. Mama didn't hire wore-out whores. There was cribs on the other side of the creek but I hated to see her go there.

"Once we get to town, Doc can look you over, then you can decide what you want to do."

"First thing, I want a room in a hotel all by myself."

"We'll get you that, and a bath. I'll have Emma fetch you some new clothes."

A mile from town, a bunch of riders came toward us and I drew one Peacemaker just in case. Turned out to be Fripp and a dusty posse. Riding drag was Papa and Sam Lancaster.

"I'll be taking your prisoners now," Fripp said in that commanding voice of his.

"No, you won't," I said right back. "I caught 'em, and I'm taking them in. You're welcome to ride along."

"Nice work, Honey," Papa said as he rode up beside me. "Three hundred and fifty dollars—not bad."

"Two hundred and fifty," I corrected.

"After you left, they put a hundred on Walton. You only get eighty if he dies, though, so we best head straight to Doc's."

"Ain't no one to do the paperwork in Fry Pan Gulch since I ain't deputy now."

"I do believe your champion will persuade Fripp to get it done."

"Champion?"

"Sam Lancaster. Seems as he's a mite smitten with my daughter. Me'n him are gonna have a set-to if he don't have the right thing in mind."

"Good grief, Papa, I only talked to him twice. And I ain't interested in no man. I seen enough men to last me the rest of my days."

"Only on account of you ain't seen the right man. Just like a man has to see the right woman. Works out best if the woman's 'right' man also thinks she's his 'right' woman. Sometimes that ain't the way it is."

"Like you and Mama?"

"I ain't at liberty to talk about that, Honey. But you might be attracting a lot of attention in Fry Pan Gulch—you're now the second-richest woman there."

Mama would be first, of course, bein's she was the only female business owner of consequence. "How come you're riding with the posse?"

"Wakum wired me, said you were out, so I caught the next train. I just now caught up with them."

"I put it in Wakum's mind to wire your pa." Damn if it wasn't Roscoe again.

If a bunch of men wasn't around, I'd have asked him where the hell he was when I was capturing Roxbury and Clem. So I ignored him.

"How far to town?"

"A little more than a mile."

Sam rode to my other side. "If you're tired of holding the prisoners' horses' reins, I'll take them. And don't worry—I won't let Fripp take your bounty."

My hand was tired—achy weary, in fact. I handed the reins to him and I swear he made a point to brush the back of my hand with his. Sorta made me feel all tingly there for a minute, but I paid it no mind.

"Make sure Clem don't die, else I lose twenty bucks."

Chapter 24

You Have A Big Horse

Emma took in Dora Jean and said she'd clothe and feed her. I sprung for fare back to Kentucky where she came from, but Emma said it'd take a week to feed her enough before she could travel, which both me and Dora Jean agreed to.

Then I went to the Tasty Chicken, where Mama stood at the door with her hands on her hips. "Took you long enough. You look a fright—haul your ass to the wash room. The water's hot and I'm gonna scrub that grime off you." Then she gave me a big hug. "You smell."

Ain't nothing finer than a hot soak in a tub with rose petals, followed by Mama washing and brushing my hair. I even let her put it up in a fancy bun with ribbons and whatnot. I'm spoiled. Whore or not, no one ever lived who had a better mama. She'd perked right up when she saw Papa ride into town with me, too, which made me happy.

Supper at the Tasty Chicken hit the spot, too. Just me and Mama and Papa at the table. Folks seemed to have the sense not to come bother us.

But when the waitress brought our apple pie, she also brought Sam Lancaster.

"What are you doing here?" I asked.

"This is a whorehouse, ain't it?"

His answer scratched up my dander some, but I shrugged and Mama told him to sit with us. He parked his butt in the chair beside me so close, his arm touched mine—seemed like the room got a mite warm in a hurry.

After Sam ordered, Papa asked him, "Where are you headed next?"

"I'll take Roxbury to Rawlins—can't do that until day after tomorrow—then head back to Cheyenne." He glanced at me, then back to Pa. "Might stop back by Fry Pan Gulch." He grinned at me. "Need to check on whether Doc has Clem Walton patched up enough to go to trial."

I gobbled the rest of my pie in two big bites, then shoved back. "Got to bed down the animals."

"What time are you going to Fripp's office?" Papa asked. "I'll meet you there."

"He don't generally get in until around ten." I started to put on my hat but realized my hair was done up. "Elsewise, he'll be here at the Tasty Chicken, more than likely."

"I have all day with nothing to do," Sam said. "So I'll stop by and make sure he gets that paperwork in. I know he always tries to charge for holding prisoners."

"And take a cut of the bounty for hisself," Papa added. "I seen it many times. Tries to do it with me even though he knows I won't stand for it."

"See you tomorrow, then." I turned to leave.

"Hold on there," Sam called. "You headed to the livery?"

"Yep."

"Set a spell, then." He got up to seat me, same as if I was a respectable lady. "I'll walk with you—my horse is stabled there and I want to make sure he's in a good stall."

I sat in the chair he held and explained to Mama. "He has a big horse."

Lancaster chuckled. "I surely do, Honey Beaulieu."

* * *

The next morning, I dressed in clean clothes and headed for the marshal's office, even though he likely wouldn't be in yet. He'd have either Wakum or Nolan watching the prisoner, so we could visit until Fripp decided to come to work.

Sam Lancaster had the same notion on account of he was standing in front of the jailhouse.

"Go on in," I said.

"It's locked."

"Locked? Maybe whoever's watching the prisoner is fetching breakfast."

"How about I take you to eat while we wait?"

I didn't see any reason not to, so we headed for Tex's Café. We ate and headed back within an hour, but the marshal's office was still locked.

"Ain't a sound coming out of there. I know for a fact that Roxbury snores like an old bear." I went around back and peered into the small cell window but couldn't see him. "He could be on his cot, but I have a notion that he ain't in there."

"Or Fripp?"

"Can't see in the office, but I don't know how he'd have got in there without unlocking the door. He ain't ambitious enough to crawl through the window."

Sam frowned. "This looks fishy. We better hunt down Fripp."

"You check his house and I'll check the Tasty Chicken."

"We'll go together. If the prisoner escaped, Fripp might be in trouble."

"All right, but I didn't notice signs of a commotion."

Sam put his hands on the window glass and took a look around the jail cell. "The door's closed but I don't see a single sign of Roxbury, either. Or a tussle."

We went straight to the Tasty Chicken, for if Fripp was in town, he'd more likely be there than at his home. I got Mama out of bed and told her the deal. She checked all the rooms and even the bathing room, but the marshal wasn't there. "Sorry, Honey."

"Look in the livery." I'd been looking right at Sam and he hadn't said anything, so apparently Roscoe decided to barge in again. He'd been making a habit of doing that when I couldn't say anything back.

"We best go ask Wheat if Fripp rented a horse," I suggested to Sam. "Maybe Roxbury escaped and Fripp's after him."

"Or maybe he's taking Roxbury to Rawlins to collect the bounty for himself."

I nodded. "The train's already left. You should have a little talk with the ticket agent."

When we got to the livery, Wheat told us Fripp hadn't rented a horse. One more thing didn't set right with me—Sassy and Pickles was missing. I hadn't seen either the donkey or the mule all morning.

"Did you put them in a livery stall?" Sam asked.

"Naw, I don't bother. They won't stay in anyway." But they'd never once run off.

Sam grabbed the bridle that hung on a nail by his horse's stall gate. "I'll saddle up."

But then I heard a bray that didn't sound none too happy, so I took off past the corrals at a run with Sam right along side.

Sassy looked like a queen on her throne as she sat on Marshal Fripp. Roxbury flew off Pickles' back—I swear that mule bucked him ten feet in the air—and when he came down, Pickles gave him a swift kick in the ribs.

"Roxbury's tied up," Sam pointed out.

"Get this damned donkey off me," Fripp groaned.

I shrugged. "Donkeys do mostly whatever donkeys want to do. Looks like she wants to sit on you right now."

"Get her off! I have to take the prisoner to breakfast."

"The hell!" Roxbury called. "He was taking me to Rawlins so's he could claim the whole bounty."

"That's because the prisoner escaped. I caught him again, so the bounty's rightfully mine. Now move your damned donkey or you're fired."

"Kiss my ass," I told him.

"That ain't funny."

"Neither are you. First off, the prisoner's hands are tied behind his back, so no, he didn't escape. Roxbury's never told the truth that I know of but my guess is he's right this time. Second, you can't fire me on account of I don't work for you."

Sam dragged Roxbury away from Pickles, who seemed to delight in giving the scoundrel a swift kick every now and again. Once he got the prisoner secured, I waved at Sassy. She stood on all fours and let Fripp get up.

We took the two men back to the marshal's office and

locked them both up. Fripp got all het up about it but I had a hard time feeling sorry for him. "I'll have Wakum let you out after we leave for Rawlins in the morning."

Sam gazed at me in his way that made my insides all mushy. "We?"

"I ain't taking no chances on someone else claiming my bounty. And that's my final say on the matter."

I just hoped Sam Lancaster didn't claim me. Ain't never met a man quite like him.

* * *

I got up early the next morning and had breakfast at Bougie's Saloon with Wheat and Sam, then me and Sam headed to the Tasty Chicken where we picked up Pa.

Fripp didn't have a chance of stealing part of my bounty money, especially with Papa and Sam watching my back. In fact, I didn't even make coffee—and Fripp's tasted like squirrel piss. Even the mayor showed up, intent on making me stay in Fry Pan Gulch as deputy.

"Ten dollars a week," Mayor Tench offered, holding out the deputy badge to me, which I didn't take. He put it on the marshal's desk and shoved it to the side where I stood. "And a house."

Marshal Fripp leaned on the wall by the stove with his arms crossed and a frown on his face. "Hell, Fry Pan Gulch don't even provide me quarters."

"You spend most of your time at the Tasty Chicken, anyway," the mayor said. "You don't need a place."

I'd always wanted to live in a house but didn't want the job, and anyway, I had the money to buy my own. Fripp had put me off mightily and I wasn't taking no more shit from him. After he'd tried to rustle my bounty, I'd told him to go straight to hell in a nut sack.

"Sorry, Mayor, you'll have to put up with Fripp," I told Tench. "I don't plan to stay in town regular." That's when I saw a wanted poster.

Wanted Dead or Alive
Boyce McNitt
$500
Last seen in Winnemucca, Nevada

That was damn close to Silver City, Idaho Territory. I could make a goodly amount of money, then visit my sister and stay until she birthed her baby. I yanked the poster off the wall, folded it, and put it in my pocket.

* * *

Papa and Mama ganged up on me and convinced me to stay in Fry Pan Gulch rather than go to Rawlins with Sam and Roxbury. They said what with Sassy and Pickles having such a tough week, they needed to rest a few days. Sam seemed disappointed that I wasn't going with him, which made me feel just a little bit glad even though that made no sense at all.

Still, I wanted to make good and sure him and Roxbury got on that train, so my folks came with me to the depot, where we met Sam and my bounty catch. Sam left the handcuffed prisoner with us while he took his mount to the livestock car.

Mama watched as he strode back to us. Just before he got to where we were, Mama whispered in my ear, "I bet he does have a big horse."

I elbowed her and she giggled like a schoolgirl, which wasn't like her at all.

"I'll be back on tomorrow's train if all goes well," Sam

said to me, "with your money."

It seemed kind of strange for him to get on that train without a proper farewell, so I shook his hand. When we let go, I still felt his hand in mine. I rubbed it on my shirt, for something must be wrong with the danged thing.

He grinned at me in that knowing way again, then turned and boarded the passenger car.

As Mama and I walked away, she said, "I think you got yourself an admirer."

Rest Your Eyes Time
Honey returns in her second book:
Sidetracked in Silver City!

Will Louisa have her baby?
Will Roscoe be a pest?
Will Pickles cooperate?
Will Honey catch her bounty?
Will Sam catch her?

Did you enjoy the first of Honey's adventures? Please write a review! Thanks so much.

Other Books by Jacquie Rogers

Hearts of Owyhee

Jacquie Rogers

Hearts of Owyhee series

Set in the sweeping high mountain desert of Owyhee County, Idaho Territory, these western historical romance novels are lively, sensual, and humorous.

#1 **Much Ado About Madams**
Six whores and a suffragist are at cross purposes with rancher Reese McAdams. All he has to lose is his heart.

#2 **Much Ado About Marshals**
Cole's dilemma: Tell the truth and hang, or live a lie and end up married? Daisy's determined to marry the new marshal, but he's wanted for bank robbery!

#3 **Much Ado About Miners**
Hired gun Kade comes to Silver City and a lady banker accidentally shoots him in the head. Then he learns that the men she shoots tend to be the next groom in town!

#4 **Much Ado About Mavericks**
Roped, tied, and... A beautiful ranch foreman and a handsome Boston lawyer thrown together by an impossible will.

#5 **Much Ado About Mustangs**
Secret lives, hidden dreams, and forbidden sex in the Old West—what's a woman of nobility to do when a handsome rancher tears through her world like an Owyhee dust devil?

Connected to
Hearts of Owyhee:

Mercy: Bride of Idaho
American Mail-Order Brides series #43

One woman bent on saving her family. One rancher determined to save his own heart. Is her love enough to save them all?

Mail-Order Tangle
(with Caroline Clemmons)

Two Dickerson sisters,
two Johanssen cousins,
two great stories!
Mail-Order Promise
by Caroline Clemmons
Mail-Order Ruckus
by Jacquie Rogers

Standalone Novel

Sleight of Heart

Sleight of hand? or Sleight of Heart?

A Straight-Laced Spinster
Lexie Campbell, more comfortable with neat and tidy numbers than messy emotions, is determined find the sharper who ruined her little sister and make him marry her. When his lookalike brother Burke appears, she greets him with a rifle and forces him to help her. Can she resist his magic charm?

A Gambler With Magic Hands
To claim the family fortune, smooth-dealing Burke O'Shaughnessy has to find his brother Patrick, despite being saddled with an angry spinster. But when Lexie shows an astounding talent for counting cards and calculating odds, he figures she might be useful after all. Can he draw the queen of hearts?

"... a fun and fast paced read with a charming and sexy hero!" ~Jennifer Haddad

Novellas and Single Reads

For over a dozen fun novellas, go to Jacquie's novella page!

About the Author

Jacquie Rogers has worn many hats before taking up the pen: a former software designer, campaign manager, deli clerk, and cow milker. Besides both traditional and non-traditional westerns, she writes romance in three sub-genres: western historical, fantasy, and contemporary western.

She grew up in Owyhee County dreaming of herding Texas Longhorns while she milked Holsteins, and with her sister and friends, rode all over the Owyhees looking for bandits and rustlers. Good thing she never found any for real! Now she calls Seattle home, and lives with her husband who is an audio-video engineer, her IT Guy, and a fantastic proofreader, but hates plumbing. They miss the sagebrush and alkali dirt, and are looking to move back to Owyhee County soon.

For a fun time, please join Jacquie at the **Pickle Barrel Bar and Books** on Facebook.

To keep up on Jacquie's latest news, subscribe to the **Pickle Barrel Gazette**.

Jacquie's website:
http://www.jacquierogers.com

Amazon author page:
https://www.amazon.com/author/jacquierogers

Pickle Barrel Bar & Books on FB:
https://www.facebook.com/groups/JacquieRogers/

Pickle Barrel Gazette:
http://www.jacquierogers.com

Made in the USA
Lexington, KY
09 April 2016